CLACKAMAS LITERARY REVIEW

2022
Volume XXVI

Clackamas Community College
Oregon City, Oregon

CLACKAMAS LITERARY REVIEW

Managing Editor
Matthew Warren

Associate Editors
Jeffrey McAlpine   Nicole Rosevear   Amy Warren

Christopher Zimmerly-Beck

Assistant Editors & Designers
P.H. Drost   Maggie Ellis   Payton Hammock

Jeff Lyon   Harli Okerlund   Mystique Quintana

Memphis L. Rollins   Spencer Tiedtke

Cover Art
Pride by Kayla Meyers

Clackamas Literary Review
19600 Molalla Avenue, Oregon City, Oregon 97045
ISBN: 978-1-7320333-4-4
Printed by Lightning Source
www.clackamasliteraryreview.org

CONTENTS

Editors' Note

We are, at last, emerging from an era of uncertainty and cultural dry dock into a world where many things again seem possible. During the past two years, the written word has helped sustain us, has helped make our world seem a little more certain. We've needed that. We need that still.

As Suzy Harris shares with us:
I hear rocks murmuring to each other,
reminiscing about the old days
when they were once part of something bigger.

We all long to feel that. To feel, once more, part of something bigger.

After months of dedicated work and collaboration, our student and faculty editors have created this collection of poetry and prose for you, our reader, to hold in your hands—to feel certainty, connection, that you are part of something bigger. Again. Welcome to the 2022 *Clackamas Literary Review*.

Helios Ave

Emma Charlton

morning makes the world look blue
and by the world, i do mean everything.
even the orange-tinted porch railing that peeks into my view;
i could see it as the sky.
thin paper birch tilt with the weight of last night's snow (not much),
the layer of snow as thick as the trunk itself.
the strong trees, the ones i grew up with,
they stand tall under the accumulated weight. encouraging.
spruce take a blue-black over their forest green.
branches of needles, comforters, dusted in fresh snow.
i can just see the sky through the trees, a true baby blue at 8:47
a new beginning.

Advice for Those Starting Out

Robert K. Omura

If you come to the mountains for peace,
be quiet! They do not need to hear your troubles,
leave those in the trunk under the spare.
Hydrate well, wear a hat, move humbly;
breathe as if your life depends on it—it does.

Start early, but not before coffee, the day is long.
You can pee in the bush. Prepare for the weather,
watch for wildlife, take photos of everything.
Avoid crowds. If a lot has more than three cars,
go elsewhere. This is not a parade.

Make love beside a kicking stream,
lay your head in a lap of crocus, red paintbrush;
close your eyes, rest awhile, the sun loves you.
The hawk and crow watch, tilt with the wind;
they will always remember you. Remember them, too.

Advice for Those Starting Out

Follow the winding trail of those who came before,
they are true, but strike a path of your own, sometimes.
Avoid the scat, sing loudly, tie your laces tight;
on the summit, leave nothing behind but respect,
take nothing away but awe; wrap it in a psalm.

How Sound Travels

Jeffrey N. Johnson

We consider the sounds of nature to be a constant,
though incremental change by year says otherwise.
On final inspection of my family estate
the bobwhite no longer clears its throat,
the silted brook has moved underground,
and the once creaking pines lay rotting on their sides,
cross-checked and entangled by competing winds
where deer gather on beds of needles to pass time in silence.
By twilight the whippoorwill have joined
their bobwhite brethren in some diminished habitat.
The trees I once climbed, the red delicious and sugar maple,
now fertilize fields of weed-choked saplings,
their cambium cells now soil for others to stand on.
Where the garden once bloomed, squirrels have multiplied,
katydids bow their legs, and morning doves cry with greater resolve.
Like so many people I know, the land had changed,
the forest transformed, but it was still a forest.
It simply shed itself like we shed our skin or change careers.
I shed no tears. I've moved on from what was lost,
and what lives on is life of another kind.

The walk away from my origin came easier than I thought,
though the sound I remember, my sound,
still echos with each weary step.

Greyhound Cowboy

Ken Post

The snowstorm hit with such ferocity the interstate between Bozeman and Billings lay obliterated in heaving sheets of snow. The Greyhound passed a tipped over semi, cars angled in ditches, and pickup trucks 360-ed into the drifts. Reaching Billings at 10:00 p.m., the bus rolled into a white-washed ghost town.

In the Greyhound terminal, Kurt watched the driver cut the engine. The driver, thick in the chest with a crew cut, stood at the front of the bus. "Listen up, everyone." He folded his arms over his chest. "Roads are all shut down, nothing's open, and our scheduled departure in one hour isn't happening." Pausing to look at his sore-backed, weary passengers, the driver said, "You can sleep on the bus but there's no heat or you can stay in the terminal where it's warm. Your choice. One more thing: you can grab your luggage now if you want. We'll reload when the roads clear."

The bus door hissed open and Kurt and eight other passengers staggered into the dim confines of the loading area. The driver opened the bus's cargo bay. Passengers milled about while the driver crawled to retrieve the luggage that had slid to the back. Out came an Air Force duffel bag for the scrawny uniformed kid with zits who said, "Thank you, sir." A young mother with a curly-haired boy around four years old waited for the suitcases the driver handed them. A leather saddle materialized and Kurt figured it belonged to the lean guy who had been sitting a seat in front of him, on the other side of the aisle. A weather-beaten cowboy hat cocked over his head while he snored. Kurt's backpack and a long plastic tube carrying his precious custom-made fly rods slid over to him. Some people carried a family bible, Kurt never went anywhere without the rods, even if he wasn't planning on wetting a line.

Everybody filed into the terminal and the driver followed them. He looked at Kurt and the cowboy. "You fellas good for now?"

"I'll make do."

"No worries here," said the cowboy.

"Good. I'm gonna try to get some sleep on the back seat of the bus." He pulled his big Greyhound parka around him and zipped it. "If something comes up, you know where to find me."

"Sure thing," said Kurt. He dropped his pack and rod case on the floor and picked up a rumpled copy of the *Billings Gazette* somebody left on a seat. Nothing on the front page caught his eye so he walked to the double doors of the terminal entrance. Outside, in the muted glow of the streetlights and neon signs, snow piled up in storefront doorways. Skeins of snow whisked by the wind sparkled in their passing. Kurt wasn't even halfway to his destination of Minneapolis to see Laura, his girlfriend and PhD candidate. The trip was a whirl of mixed emotions. The last visit vacillated between stony silence over Kurt's comment to her about scientific esoterica and uproarious stoned potlucks with her fellow students. Maybe this blizzard was an omen.

"Some storm, huh?" said the cowboy.

Mesmerized by the blowing snow, Kurt hadn't noticed the cowboy standing next to him. "Yeah." He kept facing the window. "Wonder when it'll end."

"No telling."

They turned to look at one another for the first time. Kurt saw an older guy, late forties with short, blond hair under his hat, and eyes as blue and clear as the pools stacked with trout on the Beaverhead River. He was creased from a scorching sun and scoured by cruel winds.

"I should make a call," Kurt said.

"Good luck." The cowboy pointed to the payphone with the phone receiver ripped from its cable.

"I'll use my cell phone." Kurt pulled the phone from his pocket and then set it back in. There was no use getting Laura upset this late at night. He could call in the morning when he knew more about his departure.

"Want a piece?" The cowboy handed him a stick of gum in its foil wrapper.

"Sure. Thanks," said Kurt. He folded the Wrigley in half and set it in his mouth, the spearmint warming it. "You got on the bus in Butte, didn't you?"

"Yup. Finished up on the Ponder Ranch. Where'd you hop on?

"Dillon. I'm heading to Minneapolis." Kurt slid his hands into his jacket pockets. "My girlfriend is going to have to wait a little longer—it's been three months." For the last two years he'd driven, bused, or flown to Minneapolis depending on how much sleep he'd had, whether his truck was running, or if his boss would give him more than a few days off. Last week's blown head gasket meant a 1000-mile bus trip.

"Ouch," said the cowboy. "That's a stretch. My name is Dodge." He put out his hand.

Kurt shook it, the calloused ridges and thick paw as strong as a wolf trap. "I'm Kurt."

"Pleasure," said Dodge.

The upcoming long bus ride across the rest of Montana, North Dakota and most of Minnesota did not thrill Kurt, nor did the big city of Minneapolis. Laura was always busy studying, taking classes, or teaching them. Unless Laura was on school break, Kurt always felt as if he was a scheduled appointment. He killed the long hours of the day on walks spanning miles of the city and suburbs, reading in libraries, savoring a cup of coffee at any of the dozens of espresso shops he wandered past. He'd grab a discarded newspaper or magazine and pour over it until his refill was empty.

"Do most cowboys travel by Greyhound now?" Kurt nodded toward the saddle on the floor near Dodge's gear.

Dodge chuckled. "There's a story behind that." He stared at snow blowing horizontally past the window.

"I figured as much," Kurt said. A blanket of snow hit the door and Kurt shrunk back from the blast. His mind drifted to Laura's lithe form hunched over her keyboard, tapping keys for her grad school research. He would reach over to massage her shoulders, nuzzle the nape of her neck. She would tense and then slump her shoulders, encouraging the fingers teasing the knots. "Now's not a good time," she said. He'd keep massaging until she reached to touch his hand. "Okay, but let's make it quick. I've got a lot of work to do." Kurt knew her as well as the best fishing holes.

"My stomach's growling," Dodge said. "Got some food in my bags. Like jerky?" He strode over to the seats where his saddle, saddle bags, and other gear sat in a heap.

Kurt followed and dragged his pack to where Dodge sat.

"Try this." Dodge handed several blackened strips of dried beef. "Made it myself."

Kurt's jaws worked the tough meat. "This is good. It's got a kick to it."

"That's the secret ingredient," Dodge said. "Red pepper flakes."

"Your secret's out."

"That's about the only secret I have," Dodge said. He shoved the paper sack of jerky back in his bags. "I'm pretty much an open book."

Kurt pulled a gallon Ziploc from his pack. "I've got trail mix. Want some?"

"What's in it?"

"Nuts, M&M's, raisins, granola."

"Sure," Dodge cupped his hands while Kurt tilted the Ziploc's contents into them. "A real potluck."

"You were gonna tell me about a cowboy who rides buses."

"Still want to hear that one, huh?" Dodge stretched out his long frame and parked his legs on the saddle like it was an ottoman.

"Sure."

"I'll make it short and sweet. I like fast horses, fast cars, and—"

"—Fast women?" Kurt cut in.

"I like the slow ones too." Dodge winked at him. "I had me a souped-up '67 Malibu, but I guess you could say I had an unfortunate relationship with the highway patrol and their damn radar guns. It doesn't help when you get pulled over after too many Coors. Dee. You. Eye. Three of 'em." He leaned back, staring at the ceiling, the dull yellow of the fluorescent lights cast a shadow on his profile. "This cowboy doesn't have a driver's license anymore. I saddle up my Greyhound now. How about you?" He nudged Kurt's black plastic rod case with his worn boot. "Is this where you keep your magic wand?"

Kurt's rods felt like magic wands. A whipping graphite switch, line whispering through circular guides, fly touching down light as a dust mote, followed by a piscine explosion. Each year since he turned ten, his dad had loaded the Subaru and drove them from Sacramento to fish Montana's fabled rivers. Kurt rowed his first drift boat with an outfitter's clients at 18. Twelve years later, the water still cast its spell on him like his first kiss. "There's actually two wands in that case."

"You some kind of pro?"

"I do it for a living, if that's what you mean." The pay wasn't great, but the tips were outstanding. His mental data bank of insect hatches, water temperatures, and each hole in southwest Montana rivers, enabled Kurt to coax a fish from a quiet pool under an overhanging bank bristling with willow, or a swift bend like a silver slipstream.

"You're lucky," said Dodge. "It's getting harder to find work. Each spring when the snow finally melts, sleazy realtors pound "for sale" signs at the ranches. I worked cattle on the Sparks ranch two years ago and now it's subdivided, cut up like one of those fancy cakes in a Bozeman bakery."

"I guess so," said Kurt. He'd built a reputation, fish by fish, client by client. Dudes with tech or hedge fund cash from the Bay area, Seattle, New York, or wherever it is people make so much money they don't know what to do with it. More than a few fell in love with the place and were the same folks buying the subdivided land—or the whole ranch. The hills were dotted with monumental log trophy homes sporting 40-foot river rock chimneys. Kurt's dance card filled with "repeat" clients, and some brought their daughters along.

Laura was one of them. Tied to a willow, the boat shimmied in an eddy while Kurt and Laura cast from a gravel bar. Rainbow trout with their black spots and dash of pink iridescence dotted the surface, feeding on stoneflies. Laura plopped a fly right on a big one that shot upstream with it. Kurt was at her side, coaching, praying she landed it. Laura hopped on the bank, flushed with excitement while Kurt waded into the river, netted it, and plucked the fly from the trout's mouth.

"Want a picture with this baby?" Kurt asked.

"Definitely!"

"Kneel in the water and take the fish out for a second." He pointed the camera at her, focusing on the blonde hair spilling over her shoulders. "Got it. Now hold the fish in the water until it swims away." The rainbow's gills fluttered, and it eased out of Laura's hands, disappearing with the current.

"That was amazing," Laura said. She gave Kurt a hug, and he dropped his rod on the gravel.

In the evening, after Laura's father had headed to their cabin, Kurt drove Laura in his rattling F150 to the Blue Moon, and they spun around the dance floor after two shots of Cuervo.

"Let's have another round. I'm buying," Laura said.

"I'm going to pass, "Kurt said. To utter those words tested the limits of his self-restraint. Laura stood in front of him in tight jeans, and maroon and gold University of Minnesota t-shirt. She did not look like a woman who heard that before. "I've got an early morning trip with two guys from Portland. Raincheck?"

Kurt walked back to the bunkhouse after dropping her off and rubbed the spot where she had planted a kiss on his cheek. He didn't know who was doing the catch and release.

"I'd like to catch one of those realtors in the act of posting a "for sale" sign." Dodge made a fist and held it in front of him like a club. "I'd give 'em a good shake. Half of them grew up in the valleys they are selling off faster than tickets at the county fair kissing booth. More like selling their souls." He took his hat off, scratched his head, and put it back on. "I've followed those damn survey lines, touched the wooden stakes with orange flagging, and been half-tempted to rip 'em out of the ground. I'm sick of it—I have to scratch for a ranch hitch these days."

"Sorry to hear that. I really am." Kurt saw Dodge's way of life washing downstream while river bottoms, meadows, and barren slopes filled with homes, trailers, and lodges right up the ridges. He ran his zipper up and down on his pile jacket. "I work so much it's hard to find time of my own. The season used to be May through October," Kurt said. "Now it's just about year-round. We have insulated waders, toe and hand heaters, you name it," Kurt shifted in his chair. "I have to fight for time off." He and Laura had many "discussions" about his lifestyle; she couldn't understand why he had to work such long hours. "You care more about your clients or fishing buddies or whatever they are, than me," Laura said. There was no denying he wanted to share his love of fishing with them, to see their wide grins cradling a rainbow before sliding it into the river. "What about you?" Kurt fired back. "You spend more time in the lab than some of those rats in their cages." It hadn't started out that way, but now they were like two rams butting heads.

"Count your blessings about work." Dodge settled against the seatback, putting his arms up on it, and looked at Kurt. "I don't begrudge anyone a living but this is hard to take. The dudes you take out are spoiling a good thing."

Dodge's words contained a nugget of hard truth. Kurt wasn't blind to the changes and didn't like everything he saw either: spiraling real estate prices, commandeered fishing holes, elbow to elbow at the bars. First and foremost, he was a fisherman—for his own sake. It defined him. Kurt fished alone long and hard in his off hours, hiking in blackness to inaccessible reaches by headlamp. It was a gift to find that spot where it all flowed together: the near-dawn silence, the lap of water, the first red rays of light, the accompanying chirp of birds awakening.

"I'm not in it to ruin anyone else's life. I just love what I do." Kurt popped some trail mix in his mouth. "I wonder if we're taking better care of the fish but screwing up a lot of other things in the process."

"Amen to that. As far as fishing goes, I can stick a worm on a hook and fling it out, hoping something bites," Dodge said.

"We don't use worms. We use flies."

"You mean those things that look like the ass-end of a rooster?" Dodge took his feet off the saddle and pulled it towards him, leather creaking.

"Some of the flies have feathers."

Dodge shoved his hat back on his head. "And they catch fish better than worms?"

"They work pretty well, but it's a bit more difficult because we don't have barbs on the hooks."

"Why the hell not?"

"The barbs make it hard to get the fish off the hook." Kurt caught the saddle's earthy smell of leather and horsehide. He wondered about the hook Laura set. It sure felt like it had barbs.

"Who cares? You clobber it over the head and it's half-way to the frying pan."

"Well, we don't eat 'em."

"What?"

"We let them go. It's called catch and release."

"Now I've heard everything. Closest thing I ever got to that was getting those calves down on the ground and stickin' them with a hot brand. Off they go bawling. No harm comes to them. Except for the castration." Dodge let out a gravelly laugh.

Kurt's hand subconsciously moved to his groin. He wasn't getting his balls nipped but saw his nuts in a vise over what his friend, Derek, called this Laura thing. "Sure she's hot. Yes, she super smart. But how's this going to work out," Derek asked, "with you trying to catch every fish in Montana and her staring into a microscope in Minnesota?" Back and forth they went, empty beer bottles lining up on the kitchen table, hashing out romance in general, and Laura, in particular. "Face it, you're two cards from different decks." Kurt went to bed convinced it was over. Two days later he was standing in front of the Dillon Greyhound bus stop.

"Ya know," Dodge said, "I get a lot of thinking done on the bus. Kinda get lost in the motor's drone when you're not doing the driving."

"What do you think about?"

"All sorts of things. Growing up. Stuff I'd take back. Things I wished I'd done when I was younger." Dodge's two fingers pinched his upper lip and he held it while his stare drifted toward the wall. He sighed. "When you get to my age, it's harder to change. If I've learned anything, and some would say it hasn't been much"—he tapped Kurt with an elbow—"once you make a decision, go with it."

They sat in silence for a minute and Kurt squinted at his watch: 12:15 a.m. "I'm gonna try to get some sleep." He opened his pack and fluffed up a sleeping bag and laid it across a row of chairs.

"Sleep sounds good," said Dodge. He yanked a worn Pendleton blanket from a saddle bag, set the bag under his head for a pillow, and draped the blanket over him on the adjoining row of seats. "Ya know, there are a lot of things you can change but snowstorms aren't one of them. They're beautiful in their own right, so you best ride 'em out and pick up from there."

"That's solid advice," Kurt said.

"Good night, Mr. Fisherman."

"Hope so," said Kurt. Closing his eyes, a vision of a river appeared, pouring across a rock-cobbled bottom. Ahead, the river forked, one side edging a high bank, the other trembled over small boulders scattered willy-nilly in the current. The river disappeared into the mist of sleep.

A rustling sound awakened Kurt.

Dodge was packing his blanket. "Snow's stopped. It's light out and they plowed."

Kurt looked at his watch: 8:15 a.m. "Already?" Rubbing his eyes, he felt a violent need to pee after a restless sleep. He had reawakened at 2:00 a.m. and twisted and squirmed in his bag until after 4:00 a.m. before finally drifting off. "Watch my stuff, okay?"

"Sure."

Kurt headed to the bathroom. The door sign had fallen off and somebody had taken a black marker and written "Men" on it. His piss sprinkled off the deodorizing cake. Kurt washed his hands and dried them with paper towels, staring at the nearby condom machine. Colored, flavored, extra large. He wasn't going to need them.

Dodge sat next to his saddle, his hand on the horn in a gentle caress. "They're boarding in ten minutes. I guess the roads are open. Some kind of miracle, if you ask me."

"I gotta do something." Kurt headed to the ticket window and spoke with the gray-haired lady behind the tiny frame of window.

The driver stowed the luggage in the cargo bay of the bus, but Kurt held back against the wall with his gear. A line of passengers formed by the closed bus door.

Dodge turned around and saw Kurt leaning against the gray cinder blocks. He stepped out of line. "Coming?"

"Nope." said Kurt.

"What about your girlfriend?"

"I guess we're gonna have a long, unpleasant conversation." Kurt didn't relish dialing Laura and breaking the news. There didn't seem like there was any way it was going to work in Minneapolis or any other city Laura did her lab work. It was all a box canyon for Kurt. He couldn't keep this internal tug of war going; it was easier to let go of the rope.

"Had a few of those myself," Dodge said. "None of them were fun. One tried to knife me."

The rumbling of the bus started, a cloud of exhaust billowing into the garage. Kurt couldn't alter what was happening in the snow-fed valleys of Montana where multi-hued trout were more valuable than the marbled meat of a grass-fed cow. But he was changing horses in midstream, something no sane cowboy would do.

"I guess this is adios." Dodge shook hands with Kurt. "Next stop, 150 miles east to the hoppin' town of Miles City."

"Thanks for the jerky. Maybe I'll whip up a batch." He hoped Dodge hooked up with a ranch needing a savvy horseman. "Good luck with the highway patrol."

Dodge stepped up on the bus, tipped his hat and disappeared into the darkened interior.

The garage door rattled open and a burst of bright snow-reflected light forced Kurt to squint. The printing on his ticket looked larger than normal: Dillon. Heading west. Heading home.

One Woman

Cecil Morris

She lives in Portland with her husband
and two small children, two girls who grow
magic fast and straight, her fairy tale,
these girls who will too soon surpass her
in height and reach and remarkable feet
and feats—before she even realizes
that she has become an old woman, the hag,
that she has herself begun to shrink,
to withdraw like the tide from her highest point,
her farthest reach. She goes to Cathedral Park
under the soaring arches of St. John's
Bridge hoping to catch wedding parties posing,
photographers circling, choosing angles,
framing angels, and thinks about her daughters
in white, her daughters radiant, opposite
of black holes, her daughters framed, posed, perfected.
Sometimes she walks alone across the bridge,
suspended with all the steel and pavement
and cars, high above the river, languid
but relentless in its journey to the sea.
She pauses then at the center, at the top
of the gentle arch, halfway, halfway,

she holds herself still and stills herself,
closes her eyes, and tries to separate
the voice of the bridge, the hum and flex
of it, from whispers of air moving, from traffic,
from her own breathing, from her own thoughts,
from the thousand and one nights and the blue
descending or the clouds and the future
rising, rising, rising all around her.

It Could Have Been Different

Vivienne Popperl

It all started with Eve's story. How it was told.
Here's what I remember: The garden was billowing

with greenery and song, the air languid. Adam was lying
on a rock in the river, staring into the blue.

The rustle I heard was a small bird, bright-eyed,
saucy tailed. It perched on my shoulder, cocked

its head, told me about a beautiful purple
fruit on a golden tree. It flew ahead of me.

I stopped, dazzled by purple and gold, fell
to my knees. Each fruit trembled, quivered,

sent out vibrations of song. Lines of poetry
curled into the warm air. The little bird

urged me to taste the fruit. I inched forward on my knees,
hands reaching up. My fingers closed on the soft

purple flesh, tugged. *Ooh don't pinch me!*
I recoiled, crept up again, cupped my hands,

gently tugged. Perfectly shaped to fit my hands,
the weight dropped into my palms. Singing surged around me,

a chorus. *Take a bite! You will become
a muse to humankind!* Tenderly, I raised the plum

to my lips, kissed it, bared my teeth, nibbled.
Sweet juice rushed into my mouth, down

my chin. I was filled with dance and song.
Adam stared, grinned, took my hand.

We rejoiced. We'd found
our voice.

Romancing the Rail

Steven Mayer

Weaving along the Colorado River, flowing fast and swollen, we move by rail, living out a long-imagined dream, a train trip east from Grand Junction across the State of Colorado through the Rocky Mountains to Denver. Nearly 250 miles and nine hours in length. At first, the landscape is wide and barren, but canyons quickly deepen and narrow. High snow-topped mesa ridges and sheer red sandstone cliffs soar around us. The words of Barry Lopez lift off the page of his book *About This Life*, which I am reading, "The real American landscape is a face of almost incomprehensible depth and complexity. The shock to the senses comes from a different shape to the silence, a difference in the very quality of light, in the weight of air." I sense being drawn into a mystical place filled with wonder and beauty.

"My God, we are clinging to a cliff along the river," my wife exclaims, "sheer cliffs rising next to us. It takes my breath away." She clings to me, unnoticed, her spirit never tied to the rail, her finger on the window pointing in amazement, not fear, beheld by an enduring romance of the heart. Hers is a gleeful meditation, eyes open—heart, too, as the vast horizon flows toward her with a mesmerizing natural landscape.

White water rapids in deep, narrow canyons abound, as do rafters, kayakers, playfully "mooning" us in tribute to the wilderness, exposing their wildness. I imagine myself in a kayak, paddling through white-water rapids. For me, it is a solemn ritual of old age to be young again to kayak or raft, a purely delightful fantasy. The wandering spirit of John Muir whispers to me, "In every walk with nature, one receives far more than he seeks." I am seldom bored by this place. On the contrary, the longer I am in this wilderness, the more it expands and reveals to me, details noticed for the first time, rich in texture and terrain, wedding me to this sacred place.

Tunnels along the way, twenty-seven of them, immerse us in sheer darkness, gently rocking us on the rumbling track below, igniting impulses of romance. Even this writer must put his pen aside for a kiss. I sense that fear might embrace us if not playful, as the darkness can be foreboding, especially in tunnels six miles long and on terrain with loose rocks and wildlife finding their way across the tracks.

Grand mesas fade as our river canyon deepens, snowcapped mountains rise in the distance, revealing their granite grandeur with boundless forests and aspen groves, all in nature's upper reach. The mystic is at home in the wilderness, and I wonder if I could live in a cabin, a century or more ago, surviving this hostile environment's hardships? Few have carved trails through this rugged landscape with little water or vegetation. A harsh sun relegates life to the shade. I share my daydream, and my wife shakes her head in disbelief, though I suspect she is tougher than she imagines, much like her mother, who grew up on Alberta's eastern prairie a hundred years ago. There is wise prose reaching out to us, "Those who contemplate the beauty of earth find reserves of strength that will endure as long as life lasts. Those who dwell ... among the beauties and mysteries of the earth are never alone or weary of life" (Rachel Carson, *A Sense of Wonder*). Comforting thoughts when faced with peril, but I irrationally yearn for the adventure of survival. A bit crazy, perhaps, but never in doubt.

Pointing to teetering boulders and bare-rooted trees on the edge of high cliffs, I wonder what grace of nature might prevent them from toppling upon us, derailing the train. I confess my faith is shaky, disbelieving that they have not moved for decades, if not centuries. We return to easy conversations about the trip ahead. My wife quietly hums as her gaze never turns from the window. She shares poetic words, "My life flows in endless song. How can I keep from singing" (Kathleen Dean Moore)?

Ski and hot springs resorts along our path invite new passions in another lifetime. Or, in this life, merely relaxing in hot springs, enjoying the conversations of others who find their way to nature's gift. The train is in no hurry, nor are we as we flow with rivers, clouds, sun, and shadows—nature's exquisite mosaic. Riding the rail is like wandering, not knowing where we are, never lost.

The dining car brings instant community, breaking bread with strangers of all ages, backgrounds, personalities, and wit. We are surprised how meaningful conversation and human connection arise. Across from us sits a woman traveling from San Diego to New York, enjoying the luxury of a sleeping car. Next to her is a young man, a college mathematics graduate working in Denver, who often rides the rail. We are fully alive and at peace in this place. We slow down, see more, think less, feel deeper, and prime ourselves for living a beautiful life.

Back in the passenger car and alone, the philosopher in me closes his eyes in silent reflection and opens them to "people-watching:" children running up and down the aisles, men napping, women reading, young people laughing or snacking, nearly all oblivious to the landscape after a few hours on the train, taking for granted the wonders around us. However, my wife remains glued to the window, drinking in beauty, tasting sweetness, inhaling fragrance deeply in this place. She is nearly speechless, willfully humble, ultimately intimate with all that exists here, her bag of magazines and books untouched.

Why am I here? A traveler, wanderer, companion, and lover. Alive in my thoughts and emotions, grateful to be here. Why am I on this train, on this earth, in this life, with this woman? I am seduced by the rail not to seek answers but to remain in the meditation of this place. If I do, the answers will find me.

Plato's Cave

Grace Cram

i contemplate the reflection of the heavens
in the looking glass of the sliding deck door
(corporeal light of the sun
proves too brilliant for flawed eyes).

i scroll through life
with my thumb,
streaming consciousness.

my version of the world is better—
smiling faces and sky of clouds prettier—
in pixelated square photographs.

i don't want to leave my room
because stepping into daylight
means no power to manipulate
the shadows i cast.

Flat Chalk Slates

Sarah Kain Gutowski

Because my ordinary self is ordinary, she expects
the standard story structure: conflict, complication,
climax, consequence, conclusion. And of course, a moral,
preferably with pictures. My extraordinary self
looks for vague epiphanies, pseudo-insightful tension
that crests and ends with two people sitting in room:

their large, vacuous silence; the stark cut to black;
the slow creep of final credits. Profundity
you glean days later, as you sit and brood in traffic.
A more lyric creature, my inevitable self thinks
narrative is a waste. She says the passing of days,
their story and minutiae, rarely has a point.

She's a weird Sartrean grandmother we mostly ignore,
although, out of everyone, she's probably the most right.
Sometimes a freakout is just a freakout, she insists.
Sometimes, she sighs, *we don't learn a goddamn thing.*
Most of us are flat chalk slates washed clean by time.
Dust and then the darkness. In the end, no lesson remains.

Turquoise

Sue Fagalde Lick

I

In a blue bathroom with pink and maroon tile,
a child swishes back and forth like a minnow
in a porcelain tub full of Mr. Bubble suds.
Her father comes in, growls, and waves a Cabazon,
sharp white teeth, turquoise mouth and throat.

At 13, she perches on the edge of the tub,
her mom finally letting her shave her legs.
She scrapes the razor from ankle to crotch,
watching the hairs fall off, her skin so smooth.
She ignores the stings where she cuts herself.

II

Turquoise toilet, turquoise sink, speckled white counter.
Bottles of lotion, mouthwash, mousse and hair spray,
a mirrored cabinet with Tums, bandages, deodorant,
floss in tiny containers, cinnamon and peppermint,
a sticky-edged bottle oozing Tabu perfume.

He comes up behind while she's drying her hair,
reaches cool hands inside her robe. She turns.
They kiss, leaning against the speckled sink.
The robe falls to the mat. Her wet hair dries
lopsided as the heater fan in the ceiling hums.

III

The widow kneels on the floor with a wrench,
fighting to loosen the pipe that won't drain.
She gags at the stinking clots of hair and soap
that she drags out with toothbrush and fingers,
curses as she fights to refit the corroded pipes.

She leaves a dishpan underneath for fear it will leak.
Her strongest turn of the wrench is not as strong as his
before he forgot how to shower, how to brush his teeth,
how to trim his whiskers standing over the turquoise sink,
before he stood confused outside the bathroom door.

Later, dressing for Christmas Eve, the woman
dabs foundation on her wrinkled cheeks,
squints as she fills in her eyebrows with pencil,
wonders *are red lips too much for me*,
wishes he was there to say they're not.

IV

This bathroom doesn't contain a tub,
just a shower sealed with dirty grout,
a molded plastic shell with orangey stains,
a rack with soaps, shampoos and body wash,
a hairy-legged spider too high to reach.

She doesn't sing in the shower. Sometimes she prays,
although it seems sacrilegious to be invoking God
while scrubbing between her legs. Maybe it's okay.
Wet, scrub, rinse, dry. The same with dishes, cars,
and laundry, but our skin bruises much more easily.

The Walkers

Maureen Sherbondy

The Vice President of Human Resources stared out the window from the third floor at River Valley Community College. She was once again concerned to see Jason Freeman, the only remaining Biology instructor, walking the parking lot. Even though it was raining. Even though his button-down shirt was getting soaked. It was as if he didn't feel the rain, or if he did, Jason Freeman didn't seem to care.

"Miss Smithers, here's the job description you wanted," said Irene, her trusty administrative assistant, one of few remaining employees still at the college from the nineties.

Thelma Smithers turned to take the paper from Irene, who was not only a loyal employee but was her second cousin once removed on her mother's side.

"It's going to be hard to replace the webmaster for that paltry salary, just thought I'd mention that. You know what they pay these tech graduates now? And right out of college."

Thelma nodded. "One of the many challenges lately. I miss the days of easy recruitment. Remember when we'd post a job and get hundreds of qualified applicants?"

Irene nodded. "What were you looking at just now? Another walker?"

"I'm afraid so. Jason Freeman's been out there Monday through Friday for two weeks. Since we tripled the advising load and added that new software system requirement to enhance student success. Oh, and he was also assigned the task of starting a STEM club."

Irene shook her head. "A bit much, huh? You think he's gonna leave, too?"

"Hope not. Thanks," she set the paper on her bulky desk. "Can you close the door?"

After the door clicked shut, Thelma stretched out her jaw. TMJ was causing shooting pain down her cheek again. Her dentist had just fitted her for a mouthguard to wear at night. Grinding had been going on for far too, she admitted to him. Teeth grinding happened when she actually could sleep. Lately, sleep didn't come easily. Thoughts of work raced through her head. How would she fill the three open math instructor positions? The physics instructor spot? In addition, they were down to one nursing instructor, one culinary instructor, one automotive repair instructor.

Out the window, the sound of falling rain ceased. Jason Freeman traveled his fifth loop around the faculty parking lot. He passed the greenhouse where the agriculture students learned about botany; next, he passed the animal science building where lab technology students took classes; his final spot on the walk included the new biotechnology building that was a month away from completion. Orange cones separated the construction area from the parking lot.

How on earth would she fill these positions? All twenty of them?

"This is where the future is," President Highland had announced at the groundbreaking ceremony eighteen months earlier. "Jobs, jobs, jobs. That's what will bring these future students here."

While balloons released into the humid southern air, a pain started in Thelma's jaw. Trouble down the road is what she saw as she watched the sky swallow the red balloons.

And despite the ten-million-dollar bond that had passed to ensure the college's future, no one had rallied to increase faculty salaries. When she brought this to the attention of the CFO and to President Highland, they'd said in unison, "Salary freezes. Can't use the bond money for that."

She sat down and hit send on yet another feel-good message to faculty. Maybe this would lift them up. In addition, she sent a message about counseling services available to faculty. Oh, who was she kidding? Money was the solution. These folks hadn't gotten a raise in seven years. Prices were on the rise. Hell, her own twenty-six-year-old son was making more money than these instructors. And they held advanced degrees. Doctorates, even.

Outside, Jason Freeman was now kicking a black BMW. A car alarm screamed from the parking lot. The car sat in the spot with the sign Reserved for President Highland. A paid-by-the-hour security guard confronted Jason Freeman. And then Jason Freeman crumpled onto the ground and cried.

That's when she saw them. One by one the instructors filed out of the main building, the English faculty, the Math department (the two who were left), the Humanities department, and all the others. They helped Jason Freeman up from the ground, then they all began walking. Around the lot. Students left the building because there was no one left to teach them.

That's when Thelma Smithers ran down the three flights of stairs, found the walkers, and joined them.

Small Change

Connie Soper

Tent and sleeping bag stake
a territory on the sidewalk

outside Rite Aid; a rolling life
piled under a muddy blue tarp

atop a grocery cart. Plastic bags
stuffed with empty cans droop

like elephant ears, worth
redemption in dimes.

Purple clouds bruise the morning sky
as he squats on the curb, feeds

a greasy hamburger to the little dog
tied with a rope to the base of a lamppost.

Slow-dripping rain spatters from eaves
onto the cardboard sign:

need money for food. Yes,
everyone needs to eat; a shelter

with roof and door. Everyone
needs beauty. A single blue feather,

storm clouds reflected in puddles;
or to look, for example,

onto a river wide and deep and green
where the water is pure, shore unblighted.

We all want to promise
that promise, to be a boat sailing

across this great divide
of urban wilderness; bewildered,

though, at where to begin. So many ways:
a dollar, a hammer, a broom.

To Hold Up the Sky

John Sibley Williams

Hand-me-down   sneakers hang   bodiless
from threads   lighting this little ~~city~~
country. Connecting   /dividing us, depending
on ~~politics~~ skin, a skin's ~~rewritten~~   history. My
~~dead white~~ brother   for example
& everything he killed   to stay   so lit,
so ~~terribly~~ in love   with a ~~flag~~ sky   that refuses
its own stars. This   autopsied sidewalk. This
chalkless outline.   For example,   a cart ~~detonating~~
erupting in fruit   or flowers, depending
on what's been ~~grown~~ sold.   Like ~~a bullet~~ song,
sirens   bluely ignite   an already ~~unholy~~ blue
morning.   Air continues to   (dis)place
then (re)fill   behind us.   Stars scatter.
As always, stars   scatter at the first sign of
light. & *yes*   we move like that.   Like this.
Holding   this ~~sky~~ grief   up to its mirror.
(Re)writing   the blue, red. Red, as an ~~uneaten~~
apple. ~~The skin that falls~~   ~~from~~ a peeled apple.

All around us warm shells   without an echo

of sea.   Of street.   ~~Of home.~~ My brother,

I'm sorry   tattooed all down ~~his~~ my chest.

& his dead, ~~still justified.~~   & the sneakers

that just keep hanging there,   overhead, swaying

                                                            ~~bodiless.~~

Happiness

Miles Waggener

Burning magnesium bright, an unexpected happiness
Enters the upper atmosphere, which is
Nearly impossible to miss above the crowded
Denny's parking lot, a car-sized happiness searing
Over our windshields, and you can't stop thinking how
Later when you get home and are
Asked how was your day as if
Nothing strange had happened, you'll say did you
See that happiness in plain daylight
Flaming across the sky, that city-killing happiness?
I just happened to look up in time. But what if
No one else looked up to see what could have cratered
Greater Ahwatukee and humanity for
Ever if the happiness hadn't broken apart? Can you ever
Really share an almost catastrophic happiness with anyone
Beyond saying I know what I saw? Your savory three
Egg omelet grows cold in its to-go box
And maybe the military was testing something.
Maybe what you saw was not a happiness at all.

Radio Waves

Morgan Jeitler

I was seated in his chair when Casey came to the station forty-seven minutes late with his eye bruised and his arm in a sling. A small patch of blood had dried in the corner of his mouth and his steps propelled him towards me and his place in the booth. My voice wavered as I read the ad copy in front of me, the words tumbling into the microphone without any comprehension. Casey, without waiting for the red recording light to blink off pressed into the booth. His pleated button-down shirt was torn across the seam beneath his armpit.

"I wanted to wait," I said, sliding out of his way. Nothing registered on his face. He merely took his seat while the rest of us crowded around on the other side of the glass. Concern shadowed the room until Yasmine rattled the studio door. Casey, meanwhile, pushed onwards, picking up the show where I'd left off.

A pathway cleared for Yasmine, and the clacking of her heels grew louder with each step. I'd hoped she'd continue, that her steps would decrescendo back into silence once she passed me. They didn't. When she reached her peak in volume, she stopped—besides me. Her arms were crossed, and her nose pointed through the window at Casey as he adjusted his headphones. One of his knuckles was scraped raw.

"Something happened," I said in a weak attempt at explanation.

"Seems like lots of something's have been happening these past few months." The edge in her voice, I knew, was for me. The nails from my clasped hands left reddened indents in my palms.

When Casey didn't show up earlier that morning, the fifth time in two weeks, Yasmine's lips curled inside her mouth, and she slammed the clipboard into my chest. "He's off the show." In that I heard the implicit command not to let him take the reins if he came. "He's done. Gone."

"I don't have anything prepared," I lied. I spent all of last month huddled on my couch with composition books racked with programming in a handwriting legible only to me.

"Make something up."

Yasmine stuffed me into the booth where my hands fumbled around the equipment with apprehension rather than a lack of skill. Twenty minutes in, I caught the motion in her chin before she shut the door. A nod. She nodded at me, and still, I floundered when Casey came through that door. I flopped over for him before he even asked. Of course I did.

Now, with Yasmine beside me, Casey coughed into the microphone, and I waited to see what she might do.

"Well?" she said, every part of her face pressed except for that nose pointed just between my eyebrows. I didn't know what she expected of me. The woman was unreadable; her responses were toneless one-word quips: always blunt yes's and no's.

She must've seen my hesitation. "Why do you do this?"

"What?"

"Protect him like this. You don't even know him."

"I'm not protecting him."

"Alec," she said, "that's a lie. The show you did was scripted. It was patchy and awkward, but you were prepared." She waved her hand towards the booth where Casey alone laughed. "Let him go."

When I didn't respond, she sighed. "Get back in there. You'll host together today."

When I interviewed here four years ago, we swept past the booths on our way toward the office. Through the slitted window, I glimpsed Casey behind the glass wall, leaning into his microphone. His words carried through the speakers in the hallway, but they didn't seem to belong to the man whose lips moved in time with the broadcast. Casey's face was pocked with the scars of past acne, and his clothes clung to his bones at puncturing joints. But when he spoke, when he interviewed guests and callers, charisma seemed to drip into the ears of his listeners.

I tried before to mimic him and the accentuated cadence he'd become known for. In the bathroom at home, I stood in front of the mirror with a recorder at my side begging my voice to lilt as his did. On playbacks it sounded like I couldn't cover up the drabness that was me, like it was so me there wasn't anything to cover it with.

After the morning hour ended, Casey didn't move. The dried blood still stuck to the corner of his mouth; I doubted he knew it was there. People rummaged about, no longer weary of the noises they made and all the while unaware that Casey hadn't so much as lifted his hand. Watching the backdrop of people against Casey's bedraggled clothes and bruised face, I realized no one had asked him what happened. We'd grown accustomed to his disordered comings and goings, but the wounds were new. Perhaps no one asked because we thought we already knew. He often left the building already pulling a flask from his back pocket.

"Hey," I said. "Everything okay? Actually?"

"Small car accident," he said, his voice monotone. "No big deal." He hunched his shoulders over the table, resting his head on his forearms so his face pointed at his feet. He looked like a little kid. Like Nicky.

Nine years ago, when Barb texted that one word, *pregnant*, I cried. She'd just turned nineteen and at twenty-six I had by no means figured it out. Only weeks earlier on Mother's Day, Barb posted what I saw as a fat "fuck you" to cancer in the form of a picture of our mom, pudgy and smiling. The caption said, "fuck Mother's Day." Then Barb proceeded to go out every night, returning past four in the morning drunk and high. Before long she was pregnant.

I begged her not to have this child, but she refused, promising me with her hands clenched over mine that this baby was her chance to start fresh, to redefine herself. But, of course, this baby wasn't her save-all, just another thing to fuck up while I watched.

When Nicky was born, I was mid-way through my first show, a punk-focused broadcast at the community college. He was born prematurely with Fetal Alcohol Syndrome and a cleft lip. Barb slept for an hour and a half, while I dealt with nurses and doctors and stared at Nicky in his crib. When he shuddered just once, I stopped a nurse. Barb woke up begging to hold her child, and I wished she was anyone but herself long enough to give him up for adoption. But she was who she was, and when she called me over between giggles to come look, I stood by her side.

Casey cleared his throat. The clock ticked into 1 p.m., and we were on air. Despite his lack of a full presence, Casey took callers with the same open-armed voice of the past. I saw the difference only in the expression of his limbs. His arms were plastered to his sides, whereas before they'd engaged in conversation alongside him. He paraded through, and though we were hosting together, I never had a remark ready quick enough to pull out of my back pocket.

"Caller seven, you're on the line." Casey kept the bruising of his body out of his voice well as he moved down the list of callers.

Looking back there was nothing I could pick out as memorable about caller number seven. He was maybe mid-thirties, and I remembered the audio as shaky, like he'd been walking. He spoke about nothing really—his family, his taste in music, normal stuff. But Casey perked up. His spine straightened, and he took in some of his former life.

The man joked about sharing his name with the host, but Casey's a common name. We get hundreds of callers with it and the many others on repeat generation after generation. Still, Casey's leg jittered at the knee.

"You've won the competition. Congratulations," he told the caller.

We had no competition that day.

"Oh woah," the man said. "What'd I win?"

"Two tickets to the next live recording."

"I didn't know you guys did that." We didn't. Outside the glass window, heads popped up and fingers stopped typing. My knuckles tapped against the table, but to my relief, Yasmine wasn't in the room.

This new Casey wasn't new, per se. We don't remember exactly when it started, but the late arrivals, the no shows, began months ago.

Rumors swirled in spaces he left—that someone had died, that he'd gotten a divorce, that he gambled—but no one felt close or plucky enough to prod. Even before all this, there was something impenetrable about who he was, like he stepped into a façade inside the building. He felt outfitted in a personality adjusted to the room.

Once, after I started the job, I saw him as I walked to my car. I left late and it was dark enough I couldn't see farther than ten feet in front of me. As I stepped around a poorly parked sedan, I heard muffled arguing inside the cab. I didn't recognize him as a colleague at first. He had a phone pinned to his ear. His other hand flicked with emphasis and, from what I could tell through the tinted window, his bloated face had reddened. This was a man on the losing end, a position so antithetical to the enigma I worked with, I denied it could be him. When he noticed me watching, he blew out a breath and his posture straightened into that familiar stature I saw behind the booth nearly every day.

I wondered if I came off similarly if people thought I wore a mask. I didn't share much about my personal life. I didn't have much to share, and when people asked, my staccato answers caused them not to again. I worried people thought of me as aloof.

When I left for home that evening, Casey squatted at the edge of the curb. Our building was an industrial wart, block-like and muddied brown, and Casey was beside the steel double door. He picked at the frayed cuffs of his jeans with his head bent over his lap. The scraggly ends of his hair curved around his neck to reveal a line of dirt above the collar. A few of the times I picked Nicky up from school, I found him like that, alone on the curb while groups of eight-year-olds wove in and out of crowds on the sidewalk behind him. When Nicky looked up at me, I could tell he'd been crying.

"Let's just go," he said when I probed.

In the car he told me the kids called him retarded and scrunched their lips to look like his. We took a detour to the park, and we swung side-by-side, trying to match our pace. While Nicky spoke so quickly he stumbled over his words. It felt like he was trying to make up for all the hours he said nothing at all.

I wanted to forget Casey, but in the end I didn't.

"Do you need a ride?" I asked.

With my hands on the wheels of my car and Casey seated beside me, a self-awareness crept in on me. Having others ride beside me created a comprehension of myself that went beyond the act of stepping on the gas and shifting the gears.

I told Casey I'd placed a dinner order I needed to pick up on the way back. His seat was scooted much farther back than mine. I usually left it open for storage, and he didn't bother to adjust the seat.

It was after he spoke that I recognized he'd been working up the nerve since I put the car in drive.

"Have you seen *Frequency*?" he began.

I hadn't and told him so.

"Never mind."

"Is it any good?"

Unexpectedly, a guffaw escaped his lips, and I jumped, almost jamming the brakes to the floor. "God no," he said, the laugh still floating between the words. When he quieted: "But, I mean, well, it's got this idea of multiple realities." He paused, as if waiting for some particular reaction. "Do you think those could exist?" he said with feigned nonchalance, a thin veil for what deeply mattered.

It wasn't at all what I expected. But we were both in this car, and for some reason, God knows why, the question was important to him.

He brought up the man whom he'd spontaneously given a prize to. "I saw the reactions. I know I've been a little, um, bizarre lately. But I've been distracted, focused on other things."

My mind pinged around him and what I knew of him. This was the most alert I'd seen him, maybe ever.

Once we parked, I reached for my wallet. Casey stopped me. I followed the length of his arm up towards his face and saw a determination in the set of his jaw that collided with the paleness of his skin.

In a mess of words strung with logic I couldn't follow, Casey sputtered out a vocal stampede. "So yeah, all this is to say, the man from earlier was me."

"I'm not understanding."

"It's me," he said again. Then quieter, "from another reality. I know how it sounds—"

I didn't hear the rest, because I strode straight through the doors of the restaurant, locking the car behind me. There was no more to say. He'd become disconnected from reality, and I felt culpable for letting him say it all out loud. He needed help. I wanted to rid myself of him, to let him again become that person I saw only from afar. Instead, he had become someone I pitied.

I dreaded returning to Casey in the passenger seat of my car, and I left only when the waiters' fingers and gossip turned towards me, where I sat with my prepaid meal on my lap. When I finally left the restaurant, my food was cold.

"Look, I know, I know how it sounds," he said as soon as I opened the door, "but the guy has the same name as me. His phone number is almost identical to mine... We speak in exactly the same manner. I haven't got his address yet, but I'm sure, I know it'll be the same." He went on, but I tuned it out. I didn't like that I felt like he was trying to loop me in.

"That's why you said he'd won a prize, isn't it?" I said. He ensured they'd speak again.

"Yes."

"If this Casey is you from an..." I hated that I had to muster these words, "alternate reality—"

"It is," he interrupted.

"Then why do you care? It's not you."

"But it is. It *is*."

We were still in the parking lot. Because I hadn't turned the car back on, the interior lights switched off and we waited in darkness. As he argued, he took on the form of that man I'd seen in the car, the one I thought I hadn't known when instead I just hadn't known Casey.

"But it doesn't change anything. You're still you," I said. The cold bag of food rested on my lap, and the plastic crinkled as I faced him.

"You don't get it."

"Because this is crazy." Circles, circular arguments. Again, and again.

"It isn't."

I turned the car on. I wrapped my arm around the headrest to back out. When I rolled over the curb, I cursed.

Then there was silence, and the radio became audible again. We didn't speak anymore the entire way to the address he'd given. We pulled up to a shabby apartment complex scattered with litter. A group of men huddled in the front drinking beer out of paper bags. I unlocked the door for him.

With his hand cupped on the doorway and his back hunched so he could peer in at me, he said something so soft, I didn't realize what it was until he disappeared behind closed doors. I watched as he walked past the hooting clump. A sad shape of a man, I thought, not one at all really.

When I turned the car back on, I realized he'd admitted that he needed to reach this man, this other him, because he needed to know if he still had a wife.

I didn't go into the station for a week after that, and when I did, they told me Casey was fired. I didn't say anything. Instead, I thought about the rest of the night after I dropped Casey off. I sank into my sofa, and as I ate my cold enchilada in front of sitcoms, I hoped that if there were another me out there somewhere, he wasn't eating from a Styrofoam container to the sounds of a TV show that would never make him laugh. I hoped that he lived in a world where his sister hadn't driven drunk with her only child in the backseat. I hoped that in this world, it had been Barb who died and the child I cared about more than anything else was beside me.

Repossessed

Richard Stimac

Earthmovers leveled the tract houses. Where
A grade school, now a Target. My best friend's
Home, parking spaces. Mine, a shaded square
Of green ash. The asphalted train track lends
A sense of evenness. Shadows not seen
Will not be missed. I returned to save things:
Bronzed shoes; Rosary of Mary, The Queen;
My mom's Bakelite bangles, Hobé rings.
What did I forsake? What is it I took?
Precious foreclosure, host of pawned past,
Enveloped fictions, haunted facts, I leave
Nothing. Nothing, I imagine, will last.
Reprised of memory, let me not grieve
Like tightly veiled Lot. I refuse to look.

Water Map

Paul Ilechko

There is a tracery of asphalt that covers the land   reaching out towards the borders where it crumbles into fragments

Cities are known to be stars   that reach out their tentacles of brilliance   touching at a distance

There is always a battlefield   hidden inside the quiet mystery of our forgetfulness

Ships slide silently into their positions   crossing the clouded brutality of ocean   slowly redefining the shape of coastline

These are the ports from which we launch armadas   forest transformed into the shapes of violence

Each city absorbing the currency of its frontage

Backed by the rippling topology of the land   where every window is a portal

London   or Paris   or the lurid dream of Barcelona

Everywhere the gates have been closed   the walls have been raised   a flood of fresh concrete as wide as Nevada

This is a time when water is the frontier for every nation   even the landlocked

Relinquish yourself to the shimmer of significance   ravished again by thirst.

Closure

Christina Albers

Everybody makes it seem the goal of all goals
but there are times you really don't want it.
Even after you've spent days lamenting you don't have it,
don't know how it will all end,
what will come of it all,
you want the irritation to continue,
the fever not to break,
the grief to linger,
overtime to last till morning,
even though there's work the next day—

surely there are other ways for things to be over,
something a little less final,
so that you don't have to wake up
and face what left while it was happening,
what won't be coming back,
what's gone,
and who.

Rescue Squad

Bronwyn Hughes

Bozwell had been drinking all day, and my EMT license was suspended, so we had no business answering the call in the first place. We reached the scene in eight minutes. He said he had to pee. Sure. Fine. When I found the pregnant lady, she was already in the dorsal lithotomy position with the head beginning to crown. I texted Boz, *TOO LATE FOR TRANSPORT!* This was my first delivery. I laid out the towel, scissors, and umbilical clamp for Boz and began timing the contractions. *3 MINUTES APART.* The lady screamed, "Girl, get me some goddamn help!" *Where* was Boz? When the purply head came out, my panic surged and I radioed for backup. A minute later the whole baby slid into my arms. I was afraid something awful had happened to Boz, but when backup arrived he acted like he had been in charge all along. I covered for him, of course, but I wanted to kill him.

That night my boyfriend, Zach, insisted I tell the Squad's board of directors about Bozwell drinking on the job. We were pet-sitting a border collie in a swanky waterfront home where every room smelled like pet stain remover. I tossed around all night, trying to find the guts to confront Boz privately so he wouldn't be fired. I wanted to wait until after the Squad's fundraising gala because I couldn't imagine a successful event without him. But after yesterday I had no choice. Someone might have died.

I should have demanded an explanation from Boz on the drive back to the Squad but I was too shaken. Besides, who was I to criticize Dr. Kenneth Bozwell? He was so much more than my boss at the Mobjack Rescue Squad. He was a decorated EMS hero, a deacon at church, and a retired philosophy professor. On top of all that, he was Santa Claus. The Mobjack Christmas Committee chose him every year to lead the Christmas parade down Main Street in his custom-made velveteen suit, even though he was tall and thin with slicked-back silver hair, blue eyes, and a dimpled chin. A breath mint stayed tucked in his cheek, giving him the smell of candy canes all year round.

Zach and I had lived like nomads for two years since high school, but I still hated waking up in someone else's house every morning. To make each place feel homier, Zach displayed our framed prom photos and stuffed sea-mammal collection on the bedside tables. We started our pet-sitting business to save for our own place where we could adopt all the rescue pets we wanted. He worked as a groomer at Happy Paws, handing everyone our card. The from-heres didn't need pet-sitters because family would help, but the come-heres hated to send their pets to a kennel, so Zach and I had no trouble bouncing from one fancy beach house to the next.

At first we felt sorry for our clients, who had to throw money at every problem, but it didn't take long for us to become spoiled too. Zach came out of the bathroom wearing a silk robe, smelling like eucalyptus body lotion. I headed downstairs to see what delicacy I could forage for breakfast.

I hoped wearing my EMT uniform would remind everyone at the Squad that office work was not what I trained for. During my probation, I reported to Dr. Bozwell in the business office to help with whatever he needed. I excelled as the only female from my class at

Mobjack High to pass the EMT course and get hired to work at the Mobjack Rescue Squad. From my group, almost everyone quit in the first year due to high stress and low pay, but I loved the excitement of answering the call. I had wanted to be a first responder ever since my father died in the line of duty as a member of the Coast Guard.

Zach joined me in the kitchen, dressed for work in his pawprint scrubs. "You're gonna do it today, right? I—"

"Yes," I cut him off, tired from no sleep. "Where's the stuff we printed last night?"

While he went back upstairs to get the list of Virginia rehabs, I continued my search for breakfast. I found one Dove Bar left in the freezer and wondered if Zach had eaten the rest. He was always trying to lose weight, and I was always trying to gain some.

"Why do *you* have to take him?" Zach asked, returning to the kitchen. "Doesn't he have anyone else?"

"Who knows?" I said, checking the weather on my phone. "He's from the don't-ask-don't-tell era." The August humidity fogged the floor-to-ceiling windows, making the house feel like a terrarium. "He lives on his sailboat with his cat, Brunnhilde."

"That's so sad," Zach said, eating maraschino cherries from the jar. I knew Zach felt sorry for me too, having no family left in Virginia since my dad died. Zach and I both loved his big, loud family, which is why we never wanted to leave Mobjack.

Zach and the border collie stood in the doorway to see me off. I stomped on the kick start of the Suzuki Motocross bike I bought from my EMT partner, Brandon. The bike was his graduation present, but *after* he got drunk and broke the taillight, his father made him sell it cheap. His loss was my gain, which really pissed him off. To get me back, he told Bozwell about me using a defibrillator on a fox after a hawk attack. That was *after* my two prior warnings not to use Squad equipment to rescue animals. The board wanted to fire me, but Boz protected me out of respect for my dad.

Dr. Bozwell had slipped his little red convertible into the Squad's only shady parking spot. He liked to arrive early to play ping-pong with the EMT guys before retreating into his office. My first stop was always the restroom—if I didn't wet down my short, blond helmet hair, it would stick up all day, and the guys would call me "toilet brush." The Squad didn't have a women's room, so I banged on the door to make sure it was unoccupied. Splashing my hair and face with cold water, I closed my eyes and hoped Boz wouldn't make this harder than it had to be.

When I cracked open the door to Boz's office, I noticed he wasn't playing his opera music. He loved it so much that sometimes he would stop in the middle of a conversation, close his eyes, and hum with the soprano in his low, gravelly voice.

"Dr. Bozwell?" My voice sounded warped, like I was underwater.

"Morning, Jessie," he said, scowling at his computer. He was usually clean-shaven, with a crisp, white polo bearing the Squad's logo tucked into a pair of cargo shorts. But this morning he looked rough, still wearing his navy-blue EMS T-shirt from yesterday's run, reminding me that mine was wadded up in my locker, covered in afterbirth.

Staring at the coffee mug on his desk, I asked, "Can I talk to you privately?" My heart was racing.

"Can it wait?" It was more an order than a question.

"I guess," I mumbled, disappointed not to have it over with.

Dr. Bozwell's office was knee-deep in stuff. *Interesting* stuff that he magnet-fished from the floor of the Chesapeake Bay, like old coins, oyster knives, a boat throttle from a shipwreck, a swivel pulley, and skeleton keys, mixed with *boring* stuff, like EMT shift schedules, training manuals, run sheets, and expense reports. Two trails bisected the heap, one from his desk to the door and the other from his desk to my desk. If someone knocked, he would wedge himself in the doorway to block the view and talk—sometimes for an hour.

I felt special, getting to spend so much time with Dr. B in his inner sanctuary. His walls were plastered with appreciation awards for his heroic water rescues. My favorite was the one with an inlaid photo of him dangling from a helicopter.

I had discovered his drinking problem two weeks ago. Bozwell stepped out of the office, leaving me to print labels for the gala invitations. When the label-maker jammed, I used my Swiss Army knife to gouge out the crumpled labels. In search of a new roll, I went behind his desk. Instead of office supplies, I found the cabinets crammed with empty liquor bottles. I thought he was a caffeine addict, drinking coffee all day. I picked up his coffee mug and tasted its cold contents. After I choked and gagged, a fiery scorch sank down my esophagus.

When I told Zach that night, we had our first big fight. He thought it was a huge mistake to protect Boz by keeping his secret. "Covering for a guy like him will backfire in your face." I accused Zach of not understanding Squad loyalty.

My phone pinged in my back pocket with a text from Zach. *How did it go?*

I texted back, *Haven't done it yet. He's busy with something.*

Dr. Bozwell waved me to his desk. "Jessie, I need a big favor. Can you help me erase this hard drive? I'm giving this computer to someone soon, and I don't want them to have access to my files."

"Are you sure?" I asked, knowing I would make a backup on a flash drive in case he changed his mind. "A quick erase takes about two hours, but if you want to do it right, it'll take about three days."

"Do the quick one, please."

While I downloaded a free data destruction program, he left and returned with a box of Hefty trash bags. He scooped the boring stuff into bags and piled the interesting stuff against the walls.

"What's going on, Dr. B?" I was beginning to worry that something besides his drinking was wrong. He opened the supply cabinet and raked out the empties, unconcerned about the deafening clinking noises. Then he reached into his leather satchel, opened the seal on a new bottle, and poured a shot into his coffee mug without bothering to add coffee.

While I waited for his data to wipe, I helped him carry seven overstuffed bags to the Squad's truck. I felt like I was tracking a wild animal. "Dr. B, there's something we have *got* to talk about."

"Can it wait? I need you to take this stuff to the dump." He threw me the keys. "I've got a couple of errands to run, and then I promise you'll have my full attention."

As part of my suspension, I was not allowed to drive any of the Squad's vehicles, but if Boz told us to do something, we did it. Even Brandon would break a rule if Boz told him to. Boz's authority outranked EMS protocols, board decisions, and ER doctor orders.

Mobjack had the most beautiful dump, cool and shady. Zach and I joked that it was perfect for camping. Bayberries, tulip poplars, and red maples surrounded the recycling bins. When I pulled up, the attendant, Wanda, came out to help. I flushed with frustration when I realized Boz hadn't sorted the trash for recycling. Wanda opened each bag to separate the paper, cardboard, plastic, and glass.

"Must have been some party at the Squad," Wanda said, holding Wild Turkey bottles in each hand.

I nodded, not wanting to encourage questions.

"Lookie here—throwing away unopened bills and bank statements?"

She had me pull the truck over so others could get by while she combed through the trash, taking her time to study the contents.

When I finally returned to the Squad, Bozwell's car wasn't there. I forgot to take my swipe card with me, so I had to ring the buzzer. Boz had installed an electric door lock after the board learned about the community bringing their injured animals to the Squad.

Brandon's voice came over the speaker. "What do you want?"

"C'mon, Brandon. Let me in."

He was pissed because I had hung a dead cat with a cranial fracture in his locker as payback. Before he opened his big mouth, the board hadn't thought to create a policy *forbidding* the treatment of animals, and Boz had looked the other way. Now, when people left critically injured animals on the Squad's doorstep, I had to watch them die.

Brandon left me outside like one of those poor animals. I buzzed and buzzed until I gave up and sat on the stoop in the blazing sun, waiting for Boz to return. After an hour or so, his little red convertible drifted into the parking lot, top down, rolling to a slow halt. Showered and shaved, Boz looked late for Pride Week, wearing a striped sailor shirt, sunglasses, and a scarf around his neck. *He must be really drunk now*, I thought.

"Hop in, Jessie. Let's go to the beach where you can talk to me privately."

I knew better than to get in the car with someone who had been drinking, but since it was Boz, my obedience was automatic. Boz was the one who accompanied me to Washington, DC, where President Obama awarded me Dad's Medal of Honor after Dad drowned rescuing a Navy pilot who crashed in the Bay near the Mobjack lighthouse.

The paved road ended at the sand. After we got out of the car, I couldn't wait one more minute. "Dr. Bozwell, I believe you have a drinking problem, and we need to get you help."

He gazed at the horizon for a while, weaving like an inflatable yard decoration. After a long minute, he patted my shoulder and slurred, "It must have taken real guts for you to say that."

"Don't worry, I won't tell anyone. I have a list of rehab facilities."

Assuming he needed a moment, I stepped into the marsh grass to pick up a stranded horseshoe crab, setting her down with her legs on the wet sand. We watched as she found her way back into the water.

"You're just like your father, Jessie, a born rescuer." Taking off his loafers, he said, "Let's walk in the surf. This may be my last chance to mentor you for a long time."

It felt odd to take off my steel-toed boots in the middle of the day to walk on the beach. I expected him to be embarrassed, but instead he acted like this was some sort of training for me.

As I trailed behind he asked, "Do you know what Euripides said about loyalty?"

"No, sir." *Not another philosophy lecture.*

"He said, one—" Boz stopped short and I almost bumped into him. Crouching in the sand, he picked up a piece of iron ore and brushed it off. "This'll give you some perspective—a souvenir from when a meteor created the Chesapeake Bay thirty-five million years ago." He handed me the rusty-orange fragment with his scarred and calloused hand.

I held the heavy lump, distracted for a moment by its porous crannies.

"Drinking is the least of my problems." He paused to wipe the lenses of his sunglasses with his scarf. "If I stick around I'm going to be arrested for embezzlement."

"That's crazy," I blurted. "You would never do anything like that." I checked his eyes to see if he was kidding but he looked lost. Boz was the one who saved our Squad when, all across the country, small-town volunteer rescue squads were folding due to a diminishing number of volunteers. He had applied for nonprofit status, filled the board with his come-here cronies, and organized our first annual gala to raise funds to pay the EMTs.

"You bet I did. You're an embezzler too but a much smaller one." He pressed his hand against my back to make me continue walking. "When you started using the Squad's equipment to rescue animals, the board noticed that medical supplies were over budget. I thought installing the electric lock would solve it, but the board decided we were past due for an audit."

"Am I in trouble too?" My jaw was trembling.

"Of course not. I would never let anything bad happen to you." He licked his dry lips.

"What did you need the Squad's money for?" I asked, hoping for an explanation that would preserve my faith in him.

"My own hubris, I suppose."

As he blabbed on about the ancient Greeks, my pulse raced. He had asked *me* to erase his hard drive and throw away the bags of evidence, which I did out of dumb loyalty. Watching his mouth move, I felt terror and despair for both of us.

Then, like the sudden resuscitation from a chest compression, my training kicked in. The golden rule for EMTs: Personal safety comes first because we're no help to anyone if we *become* a victim. My hero was drowning but I had made a backup of his files that would save me.

We reached the end of the sandbar. The tide was going out, leaving small pools shimmering everywhere like spilled coins. I turned back, walking a little ahead to coax Boz along. He dawdled like a child, playing in the sand, throwing shells in the surf.

Zach had been right after all.

When we finally returned to the jetty to put our shoes and socks back on, Boz turned serious. "Jessie?" He waited for me to make eye contact before saying, "If you drive me to my boat, I'll let you keep the BMW as my thanks."

I nodded. He dropped his keys into my sweaty palm.

As I drove Bozwell blasted his opera music with eyes closed, so he didn't notice when I drove past his marina, turning toward the Squad.

I slammed on the brakes when I saw a huge crowd gathered in the parking lot. Boz's eyes flew open as his hands braced against the dash. A local news truck with an extended antenna loomed over the scene. Five cruisers with lights flanked the entrance. The sheriff used his PA system to order me to proceed while the crowd chanted, "Shame, Shame, Shame." I was surprised to see some of the same people who had dropped by yesterday to flirt with Boz and ask him for favors—like the chair of the Oyster Festival, who wanted him to supply an ambulance for her event, or the member of the Lions Club who asked him to judge their Chili Cook-off.

Boz shook his head at me in angry disbelief as the sheriff removed him from the car, handcuffed him, and read him his rights. Two deputies escorted me to a patrol car, saying they needed to question me at the station. Bozwell forced a smile for the crowd, a sad reminder of how he had led so many Christmas parades down Main Street.

I finally made it back to Zach after dark that night. "Were you worried?" I asked. I hadn't checked in with him since that morning.

"I knew something crazy was going down," he said, removing the bungee cords holding the cat carrier on the back of my bike. Brunnhilde, who had been yowling in distress the whole ride, began purring when Zach held her to his chest. "My feed blew up with photos of Bozwell in handcuffs. He allegedly embezzled over two hundred thousand dollars. Wanda from the dump was on the local news, claiming she was the one to alert the sheriff."

While Zach grilled Omaha steaks on the outdoor grill, I recounted every detail of the day.

After dinner, we floated in the hot tub built into the deck, like a jimmy and a sook in a bubbling pot. He handed me a cigar and held out a torch lighter while I rotated the end for a uniform, amber glow. Then he lit one for himself and asked, "Did he ever tell you what Euripides had to say about loyalty?"

"Oh, yeah—something about, 'one loyal friend is worth ten thousand relatives,'" I puffed.

Zach's laughter turned to choking.

I stretched for my pants hanging on the railing to search the pockets for the chunk of iron Boz gave me on the beach. Handing it to Zach, I apologized for my role in our fight.

When he recovered he said, "That's okay. Where did you get this?"

As he inspected the meteorite's crannies, I sank down lower to let the jets massage my shoulders. "It's funny," I said. "This morning? I would have done anything for Boz."

Fingertips

Cheryl Waitkevich

Top of the stairs, he
Stumbles a bit. I
Hold him,
The bannister,
My phone,
The book I told myself I'd
        Open.

He's all shoulder blades,
        Ribs,
        Pelvis,
        Spine.

Each concave dent,
Each ridge
I've memorized in
My fingertips.

Most nights he slips
Under the covers
And lies
Still
Next to me and
I count each peak and valley of him
Like sheep. Sometimes
I worry he has stopped
Breathing, his body
Cool, his breathing
Aching and slow.

I worry he's suffering
His slow unsteady carriage
He barely eats.
I worry he
Will fall
That his thin bones will break.

But then, he walks over
My face. Sticks his cold cat
Nose into my eye socket
And pats my face.

I get up, try
Not to trip. I wonder how
Long we can continue
This unwinding,
Wonder when my fingertips
Learned to read death
Like Braille.

Toes

Nathan Bas

my toe hurts
is numb
and tomorrow I know it will again

and no, I'm not too tired to write in my car

What am I doing in my car?

21x15 is not enough money
neither is 40x15
maybe 50x15
sure 70x15 / what's the point?

work me every day
my wrists are already cut
by opening boxes obviously

stomach's been uhg
incapacitating months

What am I doing in my car?

driving to the lab
giving shit
in paper bags

test me for parasites
is my liver giving up?
cancer?

can I get a break? a lunch?

nothing's wrong with you
imagination sees 911 everywhere
I see 11:11 everywhere

therapy sessions cost what?
no insurance

my toe is numb
don't you hear? my toe is numb

we need you on the floor
use the pallet jack
shackle boxes
drag around

these knees turn brown
faster than the # of boxes I turn.

my toe is numb

Toes

55 boxes per hour is mandatory
skip the lunch
forget your rights
$400 paycheck

and my toes
my toes are numb

What am I doing in my car?

switch to reverse
go home and cry
my toes are numb
my toes are numb

a call awaits
a voicemail

where'd you go?

Lullabies in Reverse

Cassidy McCants

How can you know someone's body without ever seeing it?

My neighbor gets up at eight, no later, no matter the day. But she *wakes up* earlier. A couple of days a week it's porn and a vibrator—usually Monday and Friday mornings. A couple it's social media apps, the scattered buzzing of reels and Boomerangs. Otherwise, it's making songs at the cat, lullabies in reverse.

I don't know her body. I don't know if she's a woman. I don't know the color of her skin, the shape of her features and gestures.

I do know the porn sounds like lots of women, the vibrator sounds like a wand, the cat sounds like a bitch, but a cute bitch. Sometimes the cat will wake me before the sun rises with a high-pitched *mraa-ah-ah-ah*, probably talking to the birds as they rise.

She works from home, typing all day, she sleeps from home, she drinks from home. I don't know her age, what kind of lines trace her facial features or not, what kind of stripes she bears. I do know she listens to "When I'm Sixty-Four" repeatedly—a song I once loathed—and the only part she audibly sings is "yours sincerely, wasting away!" A song from 1967, a song I can only assume has at least 20 years on both of us.

She showers at 9 a.m. every day, an ability I've never learned. After using the toilet, after brushing her teeth. I brush mine in the shower, incapable of dealing with the harsh light, cold floor in front of the mirror.

But, to some degree, I do know her body. Unlike my neighbor, I leave the apartment. I walk to the corner store, grab an adult Lunchable-looking thing and a Sprite. For a long time, I thought she was always in bed by 9 p.m., but I was wrong. Some nights, about that time, out for my walk, I see her silhouette beyond the blinds, slithering, swaying, hands hovering above the skin on her shoulders, elbows, as if shedding her skin by magnetism. Dancing? I think she's a bit taller than me, a bit slimmer. Straight hair. But shadows can be deceiving.

Or do they tell more than light can? I'm not the one to say.

I've tried to leave her clues to my existence, but I'm a quiet person. "Send me a postcard, drop me a line," I once wrote on an index card, referring to the song. I snuck it into her mail slot before scurrying away. Who's to say if she saw. She doesn't know my body, isn't aware of my being, and she doesn't need to be. I'd guess she has everything she needs within her—I assume—600 square feet.

Finally, one day, I hear another's voice on the other side of my wall. But who does she know? It's muffled but also louder than makes sense. What's it saying? I lean in closer, where my bathroom is walled up against what I think is her bed.

"One moment you're too hard on yourself—like with the drinking—and one moment you're too forgiving. The skipping town." It's a woman's voice. A virtual therapy session.

"Blunt, get down." Finally, the cat's name. "I thought getting out of town was a good idea." Paws hit the floor.

"Of course. But why didn't you let anyone know?"

"No one knew me anyway." She closes her laptop. My heart sinks. Who is she? Will I ever know? Her therapist clearly doesn't.

Isn't it better to know a body from afar? I wish to do so with my own; my proximity to it does not breed or bleed love. Absence makes the heart grow, I've heard.

She eats. She eats well. A night of six carrots and six tablespoons of hummus for me, she gets Napoli's delivered. "Sausage and spinach," I hear the delivery guy say. "For Rebek?"

"Leave it; thanks." She yells through the door, shuffles.

Rebek? Rebekah? Biblical. Captivating.

When for me it's an ounce of turkey and six Brussels and three small squares of dark chocolate—you can't deprive yourself always—I smell animal fat, grease, cheese, hear popping and sizzling and clanking next door.

I want a body that has a mind that doesn't mind the extra.

As I said, I leave sometimes. There's a pool downstairs. I hate bathing suits but love wetsuits. I hate the sun, but I love food-free Vitamin D. And sunglasses. I bring a book, but I don't read because I'm distracted by the couple in the hot tub. Aren't they too warm? Can you have sex in a hot tub? I don't think they're having sex.

They start whispering, looking at me then each other. They can't see my scars from there, I know. They're tanned, showing as much skin they can get away with.

I forgot to bring water. I start getting dizzy, sweaty. If I lay my arms flat against the chair my shoulder blades hurt; if I clasp my hands over my belly my hip bones dig into my forearms.

I wrap my dry towel around my dry suit, head back up to the apartment. Apparently, I forgot to lock my door—and someone stole my weathered "Welcome" doormat.

"Excuse me?"

I'm in the wrong place. Rebekah. I freeze, or I shrivel, parched, dehydrated.

"Blunt, no!"

I wake to an empty room. A studio, after all. There's ice water at my side, a granola bar beside it. I take a sip and the ice makes my insides shiver.

My phone is on my belly then in my hands. A glimpse of myself in its smudgy glass shows the reality of my appearance: hair strung everywhere, lips chapped and wrinkled, eyeholes darkened. To boot, a sunburn on my cheeks, or at least a major flush. In walk Rebekah and Blunt. Well, in walks Rebekah, Blunt curled in her arms.

"Are you supposed to be at work?" Rebekah keeps her distance. I remember I'm an intruder and struggle to make it to my feet. She drops the cat to help but I'm upright before I can take her hand. Blunt sniffs my feet.

"I'm in online classes," slips from my mouth. I was until two weeks ago, but close enough. Also slipping from my mouth are chocolate chips from granola, which, apparently, I've scarfed down in no time.

"Here," my savior says. "Take the box." She's beautiful, but not necessarily in a conventional way. Her oval eyes are smudged with charcoal liner, the kind of eyes that look like they're always crying a little bit. Or—shit—maybe I made her cry, letting Blunt out. The one creature she keeps close.

A box of organic bullshit, I already know: tapioca syrup, cane sugar, brown rice syrup, the works. My stomach turns when I confront what I've just consumed. Where did you escape from, I want to ask her.

"Thank you," I manage, and mean it. Her feet look cozy in puffy pink slippers. "I'm sorry."

"You're okay," she says, eyes still soft. I look down on her an inch or two. "I'm sure he's trying to escape me. I never leave him alone." Her smile reminds me of the crags back at home, but her teeth are bright and shimmery. "He's the only person I want around."

"Do you—" she starts, gesturing around her. "Do you know where you're going?" She doesn't know who I am, and that's okay.

"Yes." I'm a quiet person, remember. "Thank you." I feel like my eyes are watery, but maybe it's just because I'm looking at hers, all wide, receptive, glistening.

I want to stay longer but I don't. Her gaze pierces a little. It's better to be on the other side of the wall, even if right now I feel I could fall into her glimmery stare. Maybe because I could fall into her glimmery stare. I could give her better counsel than her therapist, telling her I'm alone too, and that's okay. I move toward the door, still wobbly, still feeble and dehydrated.

"Thank you," I say again. She grabs Blunt, holds him close, a thing she can't let get away again, and I get it, because that's how I feel about myself.

"Of course," she says. "Take care of yourself." She looks at my bicep, elbow, forearm, and though I know what she's thinking about me, about my body, I feel—yes, taken care of, but not judged.

On the other side of the wall, I feel better than I've felt in months if not years. I lie on my floor, trace the box of poison with my fingers. I listen to what's behind my wall: a woman with self-manicured fingernails and kindness in her eyes. As she types away, hard at work, I eat the disgusting bars one by one. I fall asleep on my carpet there, nourished, known, but free to be alone.

You Never Know

Andrea Campbell

Looking up at winter from far below the drowning earth
it seems like death and life. If you wake up early
you will find them wrapped unbound around each other.

Up above the soil are villages where houses hold conundrums
and the people think about the ocean far away.
They watch the sun fall down and come
back up again.

The children, who were sleeping, wake and stumble
from their cradles, wondering if daylight is a kingdom.

Look for me. River run I'm traveling.
Spring is just a glimmer on the map, so far away
it sends a signal like a church.

I hammer down the nail, a servant of the journey.
There is no time for home.

Struwwelpeter

Greg Nicholl

As kids our bodies know the best course, know
when to jump the exposed root, the fastest route
home through the thicket at night. Know eyes
glare from behind gnarled branches of hemlock
and cedar, even if we are told they do not
exist. Know maybe it wasn't wise to stow
away in our father's parked Oldsmobile at dusk
where ovate mushrooms sprouted from the mildewy
backseat as we listened to the 8-track warn
of a stranger in the woods who sang songs
in backward words and professed the best way
to catch a lark, his hair as red as rotten leaves.
My own hair growing brittle at four when I
refused to bathe, afraid of drowning in even
an inch of water, dirt collecting under my nails.
Just like der Struwwelpeter whose finger-
nails prevailed uncut for almost a year. On the cover
of the children's book, his arms and feet are splayed
as if awaiting a grisly hug. What we forgive
as children: a chest full of infected toys tossed
onto a fire, one rabbit spared.

A roly-poly kitten
slathered with butter by voracious rats
then covered in dough. The boy who fell asleep
only to have the room morph into a kitchen
where he ended ass-up in a bowl of cake batter.
Or it was a forest infested with wild beasts. The path
to our own house fortressed by an acre of trees.
Uproot the brambles. Conjure your best spell.
Avoid eyes that follow no matter where you run
until you find yourself back in the car, with nothing
but the smell of mushrooms and the glow
of the dome light overhead as it slowly begins to dim.

It's All Borrowed Time

Kristel Rietesel-Low

Even the far-off small cliffs and dried yellow grass
And especially the egret that sails across an arc we all watch
Until some child exclaims: *Bird*. The breathlessness

Of swimming through murk, the bottom of lake
Disappearing to girls' masks to cold drop-off.
And soon school and mornings that never lose breath-frost.

The blue ceiling darkening with inverted heat out of reach, reeds
        ruffling
Under hills of eucalyptus that disappear in wisps
To reappear again as arching canopy. The lake

Like a platter: little boys and girls at the edges
In puffed up swimmies, the little girl
Ordering boys to follow their own rules. The high drone of planes

Refracted and reappearing as bees in coyote brush
And sage. From the slow blink of shade
From elsewhere, beyond the ringing theater of small cliffs

And half-rhymes of lakebed. Taking
The beach as it covers my legs
Then feet into things we can see less of,

Lifeguards training the last hour—
The victim is—I hear as they slide a surfboard across the smooth sur-
      face
Until closing time. The little girl proposes her own canals

In the sand now, until the fog comes, the color of the egret
Standing where sand turns to algae and mud,
Erases the hills straight on, blindfolding us into night.

The Room Downstairs

Laura Remington

Carly's laptop pinged a thirty-minute warning. Sip Cocktails. Friday at five. The weekly cul-de-sac gathering had become the height of her social calendar. The thing that most resembled life before lockdown—life outside a box on a computer screen. She slapped up an out-of-office message and logged off before her boss could launch another late Friday faux crisis. Sympathetic to his subconscious need to stay in touch with the team over the weekend, she would still manage the timing of her participation.

After ten minutes of attempted meditation (part of HR's recommended pandemic health regimen), she turned off her phone's silencer and checked for any calls or texts. Her husband, Joel, an ER doctor, had volunteered to fly across the country to work in a hospital in Queens for a month when the Bay Area appeared to have flattened the curve. No missed messages.

She changed from exercise clothes into jeans, but denim felt like a straightjacket compared to the world of stretch she'd been living in. When she switched to a flowing skirt, the forest on her calves almost sent her back to jeans, but she followed HR's advice to focus on the positive—aside from the fact that no one would care, socializing more than six feet apart meant they wouldn't even know.

She opted for a glass of rosé, grabbed her concert-in-the-park chair, and walked down the driveway. From their perch directly across the street, Susan and Sam waved. A bass beat leaked out of their house, overflowing with adult children who'd returned home when their jobs evaporated and schools moved online. The rest of the group was arriving and setting up at the end of their driveways to form a semi-circle in the street.

"How's Joel doing?" Sam asked.

"So far, so good." She and Joel were the newbies, having moved from San Francisco to the burbs not long before the virus took charge. They'd met the neighbors and gotten advice on restaurants, hiking trails, that sort of thing, but never had a real conversation until Becky sent out invitations for the first gathering three weeks before. Now these strangers were becoming pandemic friends.

"Casual conversation starters have a whole different meaning now, don't they?" Becky set up well-worn soccer chairs next door.

"No kidding." Her husband, Mark, joined her. "'How are you?' for one."

It wasn't lost on Carly that the subtext of 'how's Joel doing?' had shifted from an offhand greeting to a sincere inquiry.

Russell dragged two chairs down the driveway on the other side of hers and collapsed into one.

"Night duty?" Carly asked.

"Is it that obvious?" A top-line chef, he'd become the primary parent when his restaurant closed. "Not just different meanings, but different questions. Like 'what do you do?' is history. Now it's 'do you still have a job?' or 'can you work from home?' or 'did you score a loan?' Depending."

"How about 'got your stimulus check yet?' or 'unemployment?'" Sam added.

Brad, baby strapped to his chest, delivered a glass of wine to Russell but stayed on his feet, swaying to the neighbors' music. Carly suspected Brad would be the more natural caregiver if he weren't doubly busy keeping IT rolling for a bunch of people not used to working from home. Carly wanted to hold the baby, smell her head, sway with her, but she focused on the chill damp of her wine glass instead. There would be no holding any babies any time soon.

"Joel checks in every day," Carly said, "but this past week, he's been so exhausted, he mostly texts thumbs up and snore emojis." She glanced at Becky and Mark and decided not to add details of the carnage Joel had described. Their children were on the front lines.

"We know those emojis," Becky said. "And the silent scream and fever ones too." Their paramedic son had tested positive and was in quarantine with—knock on wood—a mild case. Their daughter, a respiratory therapist, was still okay.

Everyone chimed in with some form of good wishes to Becky and Mark as Marcy settled into the final slot with her margarita. As always, she appeared camera-ready. Even her highlights still looked good, at least from a distance. A full-time lawyer and mother of three school-aged children, it was a puzzle how she exuded such good-natured calm. Her ex lived in LA, and they agreed both he and the kids should stay put for now.

"Which do you want first?" Marcy asked. "Cooped-up kid stories or lawyers run amuck?"

"Kids," Mark said.

"They're on a mission to create a video adorable enough to make it onto James Corden's show. Why they picked that one, I have no idea." Marcy launched into an amusing description of their latest Rube Goldberg failure.

The Room Downstairs

Kids. They all had kids. Even Russell and Brad. In their case, a baby born to a surrogate in Ukraine. In the midst of a global pandemic, they'd gotten a flight in, secured the necessary paperwork, and managed to find a flight out before travel and border restrictions made it impossible. Now, surrogate babies were piling up overseas, no way for would-be parents to claim them.

They all must be wondering why she didn't have any. It was no secret that kids were the only reason to move to a place like this. At least this group didn't torture her like her own parents. Joel's were even worse, not just hinting but badgering her about giving them a grandchild as if it were an overdue debt.

She'd been pregnant when they moved in. Not far enough along to have told anyone. Then COVID-19 arrived, Joel left, and the baby followed. She hated the phrase "lost the baby," with its connotation that it was her fault. Like she'd just set it down and forgotten about it. Now she was more alone than she'd ever been, less than a person, a mere fraction. She took a deep breath and searched for a positive thought. If ever there was a time it was a plus to be able to drink, it was during a pandemic.

She turned to Sam and Susan. "Are you going nuts with the clan under one roof?"

"Not at all," Susan said. "I never dreamed we'd have the chance to be together like this. It's like something from another century. *Little House on the Prairie*, except with electronics and a lot less manual labor."

Carly suspected it would drive her nuts to have to shift her life suddenly to accommodate a crowd, which probably meant she wasn't ready to be a mother anyway. A baby wasn't a crowd, but it required a lot of accommodation.

CLR | 83

"Cheers to family togetherness," Mark raised his beer bottle. Carly joined in the cheers but wondered whether it made sense to have a baby at all. After decades of love and worry, Mark and Becky's children stood in the crosshairs. Even if science found a way to control this virus, a child would be fodder for future viruses or murder hornets or atomic weapons, or plain old climate change.

Susan added, "of course, it would be nice to have a little more space. We could sure use that extra room you have downstairs."

"Who, me?" Carly asked. According to their realtor, the ranch houses on the street had all been built with identical floorplans in the early 60s—single-story dwellings with no basements. Most had been remodeled at least once since, and Susan and Sam had added a second story. "I don't have a downstairs."

"Not a full floor," Susan said, "but there's a room downstairs."

"No way." Maybe Susan was starting to lose it.

"I saw it once. We're talking twenty, twenty-five years ago. The Millers." Susan looked around. "Anyone remember them?"

"We go back to 2000," Mark said. "Don't remember them though. Whoever was there left a year or two later, and the next owners remodeled and flipped the house. Barely saw them."

"The Millers grew vineyards on the slope in back," Sam said. "Pinot grapes. Wine wasn't half bad. Got a bottle every year as a neighborhood holiday gift."

"Where was the room?" Carly asked. "The stairs?"

Susan closed her eyes. "When you walk in the front door, take a right through the living room." She pointed the way. "The stairs are at the end of that hallway." She opened her eyes. "It's partly underground with windows high on the wall looking toward the back."

"There's a crawl space," Carly said. "But it's not a room. You can't stand. And no stairs, just a trapdoor in a closet."

"Maybe they used the crawl space as a wine cellar," Marcy said, "and that's what you're thinking of?"

"No." Susan's voice was firm. "I can still picture Michael Jordan posters on the wall over the bed and smell the hint of weed. I can't think of her first name. We didn't socialize with them. We were just starting a family and their kids were older. Everyone so busy with their own lives. Mrs. Miller—whatever her name was—probably showed me the room when we started planning our remodel."

"The place was a construction site when we moved in," Mark said. "They took out the pool. Maybe they filled in the room."

"But why?" Marcy asked. "Why would anyone remove square footage from California real estate?"

"Maybe you have downstairs neighbors you don't know about," Brad said. "Think *Parasite*."

"Or Jane Eyre," Becky said. "Someone's locked in there."

"Come on people," Marcy said. "We're thinking skeletons, right?"

After cocktails, Carly walked around the back of the house but found no sign there had once been windows to a downstairs room. Inside, she stared down the hall, trying to imagine a staircase instead of the antique wardrobe filled with towels and linens. The wardrobe was too heavy to move by herself, and even if she could, she knew it would show an ordinary wall. They would have noticed a door or even a walled-off staircase when they moved in, wouldn't they? She knocked on the wall on either side of the wardrobe and on the floor, trying to hear the hollow sound of a stairwell and room beneath.

Unable to distinguish imagination from reality, she decided it was dinner time.

The scent of Indian spices filled her house as she heated leftover takeout. She ate on the couch enjoying the heat, spicy enough to make her nose run because she didn't need to accommodate Joel's preference for mild—one small silver lining. The third season of *Monk* played on TV. When her phone finally dinged, it was Joel sending a "thumbs up" meaning he was alive and didn't have the virus so far as he knew, but was too tired or shell-shocked to talk. She watched two more episodes, snacking on homemade snickerdoodles, before turning in.

When she lay down and closed her eyes, the room hijacked her thoughts. On the positive side, it was nice to have something new keep her awake for a change. Was the room a figment of Susan's imagination or was it right below her? What was inside? If it once was and now was no longer, why? After testing every possible sleeping position and punching her pillow into a coma, she remembered she'd forgotten to check back into work. She got up and logged on. As expected, her boss had manufactured a weekend project. She made a cup of peppermint tea and manipulated data into a second set of pie charts and graphs to answer his new questions. She sent the draft to the team with a note saying she was available anytime to discuss.

Saturday brought another emoji from Joel, but on Sunday, he called, exhausted. It didn't feel like practicing medicine, he told her, when you ran from one emergency to the next and no matter what you did, so many died. He'd never felt so ignorant on the job. There was so much they didn't know about this virus and they needed answers fast. Plus, with so many doctors out sick, they'd asked him to stay longer.

She filled him in on the downstairs room. The mystery seemed to perk him up. "A secret room would mean we made the real estate coup of the century," he said. They talked through possibilities and strategies to dig for information in the longest phone conversation they'd had since he left.

Before signing off, he asked, "How are you feeling?"

"I'm fine."

"Really?"

"Really." She'd never get away with that in person, but it wasn't hard to lie on the phone, especially to someone who wanted so badly for her to be fine. When it had happened, one week before her three-month check-up—the one after which they'd planned to tell everyone— he offered to fly home, but she insisted he stay. There was nothing he could do here. There, he was saving lives. Her doctor assured her she was healthy and they could try again in a few months, and reminded her they'd waited to tell people for the very reason that first-trimester miscarriages were so common. She never doubted that, but she'd un-derestimated the price of being entirely alone with the emptiness. No Joel to hug the sadness out of her, no hugs from friends or family, not even a work crew to hang out with and take her mind off herself.

When she reached someone at the city planning department, the wom-an said the computer database on residential projects went back only to 2002, but Carly could try the office when they reopened at some unknown future date. The man in the county permit office mumbled to himself while he looked up permits for the address. "Sorry, nothing about a sublevel room. Course that doesn't mean there's no room. Just no permit."

Between meetings, she posted a note on Next Door asking if anyone remembered the Millers at her address back in the 1990s. Then she logged onto her third virtual meeting of the day, changing her background to a photo of the Warriors to match the declared theme (favorite sports teams). After her presentation, she was able to multi-task.

She checked Next Door and found a response. *You should talk with Jean Rose. She knew everything about everybody. Lives in Arbor Manor now. In her 90s. You'll need to talk in person to have any chance of communicating.* Another COVID-19 roadblock. Old folks' homes allowed no visitors. Hopefully, Mrs. Rose would make it through the pandemic. But Carly wanted answers now. Sifting through e-mails, she clicked on a new one from neighbor Becky with the title: "We're here."

Don't worry about us when you want to talk about Joel. We know what's going on. Hearing about people like him on the front lines makes it better for us, not worse. When you want to talk about him or anything else, we're here. Stay safe, B

Carly left the meeting to wipe away tears and grabbed a sparkling water as an excuse before rejoining. She'd been telling herself she was protecting them by not talking about Joel, but it was herself she was protecting. When she focused on him in that combat zone, a chain of dark thoughts formed link by link. Her loss was so small, infinitesimal compared to what Joel and Becky's kids faced. People around the globe sick and dying with no family by their sides. He'll get sick. He'll die. Alone. She'll be alone. She couldn't bring a baby into this world.

She wasn't ready to talk.

At Friday cocktails, spring filled the air with pollen, causing sniffles and scratchy throats and fear of what those symptoms might mean. Brad's elbow sneezes led to a discussion of what would happen if you sneezed or coughed in a grocery store.

Carly updated the group on her research and they tried to come up with reasons to fill in a room. Water leaks and mold seemed plausible as did poor construction of a non-permitted room. Carly pumped Susan and Sam for more information. Did they remember the contractors? Realtors? Any idea where the Millers went when they moved? How about the next owners after them?

They shook their heads. "Drawing a blank," Susan said.

Marcy said, "My little darlings made me dinner last night. Good lord, what a mess." She rolled out a description, and her darlings leaned out the window on cue and waved, the youngest one blowing bubbles that floated toward the street before popping.

The group compared lengths of buzz cuts among the men except for Sam. "I can't afford to give up any more than necessary. Meet my barber." He pointed a thumb at Susan, who sat up straight. "I have an idea." She disappeared into the house while the group discussed the assorted facial hair around the cul-de-sac, giving top-grade to Russell's 70s-inspired sideburns. Susan returned holding a booklet. "Swim club directory. I used to give the boys buzz cuts for swim team. Here we go. Michael, Mary, and Marjorie." The parents' names were listed too.

Over a dinner of frozen pizza, Carly searched for information on the Millers but found only a funeral announcement for the mother from 2018. It listed Marjorie, with a married name and living in a nearby town, as a survivor.

That night, Carly dreamt her house—dream logic said it was her house even though it didn't look anything like it—was filled with people hugging and talking and laughing. Plumes of spikey, brightly-colored, virus balls shot from their mouths and floated through the air like bubbles, popping when they landed. Brad handed the baby to her, and she held the warm bundle tight and inhaled her (she smelled like cinnamon) before she remembered it wasn't ok. She tried to wave the virus bubbles away, but they kept landing on the baby, a spray with each pop. She shouted to everyone to leave, but no sound came out. Then the baby was gone and Joel—lush hair buzzed and sporting a handlebar mustache—pushed the wardrobe aside to reveal a door. The partygoers now wore scrubs and masks and lined the hallway clapping as she walked between them, but when she grabbed the handle, the door turned into a wall and fire alarms went off. It took a while for Carly to wake up to her phone alarm, and longer still for gratitude to rush in when she realized she hadn't actually hosted a deadly gathering.

After breakfast, she prepared a shopping bag with a roll of toilet paper, a bottle of hand sanitizer, and the rest of her snickerdoodles, and included a note: *Hi Marjorie—my name is Carly Nelson. I live in the house you grew up in, and I'd love to talk with you about what the house looked like back then.* She considered going into more detail, but her gut said to keep it simple for the best chance of success. She closed with her phone number and e-mail address. After placing the bag on Marjorie's doorstep, she rang the bell and stood back several feet. The door didn't open.

Three days later, Marjorie called. "What did you want to talk about?"

"My neighbor says there's a downstairs bedroom in our house, your old house, or at least there used to be. But there's no sign of it now."

Silence.

"If there was a room, the real mystery is what happened to it. I mean how do a flight of stairs and a bedroom disappear? Of course, you might not have any idea what happened later, but you must know whether it was there to begin with."

After a pause, Marjorie said, "There was a room. Michael's room."

The question of what happened to it hung in the silence. Carly thought it would be better not to push.

"I'm sorry," Marjorie said. "I thought—I can't help you." The line went dead.

Susan wasn't dotty. There was a room, and Marjorie didn't want to talk about it. But why? Did Michael commit suicide in that room? Kill or molest someone? Do so many drugs he wound up on the street? Drown in the pool? Did they destroy the room to cover something up or to try to forget?

On Thursday, Joel called on Facetime for the first time since his arrival in Queens. He was clean-shaven (no mustache, handlebar, or otherwise), but he really had buzzed his hair. She wanted to reach out and smooth away the mask marks on his face. Yesterday, he told her, things had gone exceptionally well, but they assumed it was just a lucky blip. Today was different. Multiple patients extubated and a few long-termers discharged. There were even empty beds in the hospital, so the ER patients no longer piled up waiting. They still had more questions than answers, but they were learning techniques that made a difference and every bit of new knowledge would save lives.

She could hear the distant light—the one from the end of the tunnel—in his voice.

"How are you?" he asked.

"Better," she said. "Not all the way, but better. Obsessing about the room mystery probably helped. Gave me something to focus on besides work and worrying about you."

"How's your research going?"

As she brought him up to date, she realized her room research was a lot like her boss's weekend fire drills. Not necessary for its stated purpose, but useful in another way.

It was Friday again. Thirty minutes to cocktails. Joel was in a hotel awaiting negative test results before flying home. She replied to Becky's e-mail. *I'm not ready to talk—afraid I'll jinx his return, but it means a lot to know you're there. And thanks for setting up the weekly get-together. Turns out interacting with humans in corporal form makes the world feel less dangerous. Call me slow (I say preoccupied and I'm sticking to it) but I only just got that Sip stands for shelter-in-place. Ha! Sip Cocktails. Good one. See you in a few, C*

Carly pulled a wine glass out of the dishwasher and stopped in front of the refrigerator. She lifted the magnet to removethe photograph of her eight-week ultrasound with its raspberry-size nugget and tucked the picture into a blank pocket journal.

At cocktails that night, she would give the neighbors her last report on the mystery of the downstairs room. Tomorrow, she'd reach out to Marjorie again, not seeking information, but to offer her a friendly ear in case she was alone. Even after all these years, Marjorie wasn't ready to talk about the room, and that was her choice.

Carly was done searching. She knew what mattered. The room was real. Not a figment of imagination. It was there and then it wasn't. She believed something bad had happened, but she no longer felt the need to know what it was.

Rock Paper Scissors

Saramanda Swigart

When I came in you would flee my hands
your cage hadn't space to hide from my violence
I did not hate you—but I did hate
and you were weak, pink tail, hunched shoulders
slinking abject as I felt, heart rattling at the sound of
my tread, a prey animal without escape or recourse

just holding onto life until the day I beat it
out of you. I threw you against the headboard of
my parent's bed, hate uprising,
a bloody ocean swell, unstoppable tide of
weakness (I borrowed my power from you)
and a part of me preferred to be manhandled

than left always alone in that house with the
orange wall-to-wall cut to a different home,
the sound of cello music
from the piano room with flokati rug and sweet
birdsong outside, my father playing his cello
within his impregnable seclusion the

portable *alone* he carried like a snail shell
when he was home (he could be home and never found
had secret spots to hide and curl
into that nautilus, his mind, an inward-turning eye)
my mother either gone or a weather system,
crashing storms through the house, enraged with pain.

I do not know if you had a name—if I knew
I would call you that name, and honor you
and force myself to *see* it,
that you died thirty minutes after the throw that
stopped my own heart for a year, that forced empathy
burning down my throat, the first sense of *unfair* and

the terrible knowledge that evil lurks inside too
and even now you haunt my ribcage, not prey
but feral red-eye hunter, gnawing
my conscience, your whip-tale flicking my cheek
at 3 a.m., the barbed-wire hour, when I wake and
drown in a swill of sins, there you are—back then

my ears pricked at the heaviness in her tread
anger throbbing, orange carpet unscrolling through
the house: I scrambled to safety
in another part of my cage and half the time I pined
for her, and half I evaded her gale-force sadness
she unleashed because I was there, and weaker,

the way you were there and absorbed my hate
we three, a rock-paper-scissors in that house,
though yours, the losing hand,
meant you died so she and I could survive each other
so my grandmother's suicide, grandfather's abuse—
its black hole suction—did not swallow me whole.

I'm sorry, friend. Can we be friends?
I hope your small innocent soul is free of cages,
and that you have enough space
to hide and love—and to trust—if you want to.
I hold it out to you, like a delicacy, on my open palm:
Sorry. So sorry. So sorry.

After All

Shilo Niziolek

Mirror, mirror on the wall / I catalog my parent's house: take photos of the mugs my mom uses / as I use them / sit in the spot where she normally sits / read my book where she normally reads.

It's pandemic season / my parents drove to Idaho to meet my new niece / I haven't spent a day in this house since summer / eight months ago / when the numbers weren't / as bad / but the stench of fear / clung to our shorts and tank tops and sunhats / like wet laundry left in the washer.

I am in my mother's house / I am not my mother / my mother is not here. I pet her dogs / collect chicken eggs in her wire mesh basket / say "Hello, goats," in her voice. Mirror, mirror / on the wall / I brush my teeth where my mom brushes her teeth / I stand in her shower / look down at my mom-like toes.

What is the difference between / where I am / what I am. I am / *being* mothered by her things.

Her quilt lays across my lap / I peek into her office / look at her story-board on the wall / sit where she types / type where she types. Look / in the mirror / and there, my mother's most recognizable face;

I am 31 / when my mother / was 31 / I was ten / what ten-year-old daughter / isn't enamored with/ her mother's face? I blink / blink / but here / still I am / unmoored in my mother's silhouette.

I text her while inside her home / where she isn't / tell her about the woodpecker / tapping on her tin barn roof. *That's probably a flicker /* she replies / *that's how they chum in a mate.* I stand at her window / wonder if neighbors see / my shadow / believe nothing / amiss.

Mirror / mirror in the glass / I, my mother's image / trudging in her / rain boots across rain-soaked grass?

The Sin-Eater

Robert K. Omura

At breakfast, she said she'd dreamt her teeth fell out,
one by one, and they tumbled to the floor with the clatter

of pearls fallen from a broken string; and she'd reached
for them but they rolled away from her like a dozen years.

Those years were wafer-thin, a fragile communion, into this,
and the paper tigers gnawed her fingers to the bone,

so she'd bathed all night to drown them, their hungry flesh,
their bloody breath, until even the silence blistered her skin.

She'd never said much, she'd tied her words tight as a bodice,
smothering them blue, like an unborn child; beating back

the Paris moon, the bottle, the drunken nights and the dark;
until she'd surfaced from the catacombs, death still inside of her.

Later, she'd heaved up seven pomegranate seeds, a white heifer,
the absinthe freshly squeezed from the flower of her youth,

but death had latched its claws to her spleen, refused to
let her go. So, day in, day out, she'd made a ritual of healing.

This is how she blew into my life, the sin-eater, this whirling
dervish, eating, purging, wrestling with the wound inside of her.

Sometimes, when she cracks a carrot or chews a berry,
her smile catching me by surprise, I think, maybe, she has won.

Life on the Edge

Michael Washburn

The whole city was about to go up in flames and thousands of people were likely to die in the course of riots over the beating of Jermaine Wilson, a local black man who'd attempted to carjack a Chevy driven by two UCLA athletes and had ended up with severe cranial injuries. People nervously awaited the verdict in the athletes' trial. In the midst of all the anxiety, Professor Martin Russell sat under an orange umbrella outside a café on Santa Monica waiting for his younger colleague to show up. Tourists passing by on the boulevard with earnest and eager looks reminded him of his observation, a few weeks ago, that for people who live in a place, it's simply where they live and they have to deal with the crap in their lives, while for people who yearn to visit it's a magic location filled with wonders. Professor Russell had voiced this observation to his colleague, Professor Peter Hughes, during lunch at the same café, but of course he hadn't used the term "crap." He belonged to a generation of academics uniting radical politics with the demeanor of the gentleman-scholars of another era. At times, it might have been hard for someone less well-bred than Professor Russell to keep up this courtesy during his talks with Professor Hughes, for even though they enjoyed each other's company, their conversation grew out of tensions between the complex ideological and personal differences that mark all history, sociology, economics, and political science departments. Professor Russell was a Marxist who eagerly applied the analytical tools of that school of thought to issues and problems here in California. His younger colleague, nominally a leftist, often disagreed with him. It was, Professor Russell knew, quite possible that the clashing of wits made their friendship possible rather than vice versa; he needed someone to feel superior to, and since it takes decades to develop a sophisticated knowledge of any culture, civilization, or period of history, he had a natural advantage over his colleague, as Socrates to Plato.

At the same time, he occasionally had the feeling, around Professor Hughes, such as a parent might have toward a precocious child who casts a longer shadow, so to speak, than the parent ever did. Though Professor Hughes occasionally asked about his older colleague's involvement with the arts council, he often gave an impression of absorption in his research. He was off on his own trolley, as it were. The younger professor's most vehement quarrels were with the Freudians, but he also had a caustic take on the literary theories of Jacques Derrida and Helene Cixous and the cultural/economic analyses of living scholars like Mike Davis.

But that wasn't what really bothered Martin Russell. The last time he'd met with Peter, the younger professor had brought up a disturbing case that unfolded in Quebec. It was the case of a doctor in early middle age who grew distraught at the breakup of his marriage and tried to commit suicide. Upon swallowing windshield wiper fluid, the doctor decided he didn't want his small son and daughter to live with the horror of seeing their father die, so he grabbed a knife and hacked them both to death. The doctor survived, his children did not. But the most incredible thing, in the view of some observers, was yet to come. A jury of seven women and four men found the doctor not criminally responsible for his actions. They listened to his lawyer's arguments that his behavior plainly showed he was not in his right mind, and therefore not guilty by reason of temporary insanity. Professor Hughes voiced shock at the verdict. Nobody who commits murder is being reasonable, he argued, but the clinical definition of insanity encompasses a state of mind in an altogether different category from the state of jealousy and anger motivating the doctor. Clinical insanity was not in evidence here.

"Could you arrive at the point, Peter?" Professor Russell said.

"I should think my point is obvious. What we see in this case is a kind of Alice in Wonderland logic: the more heinous your crime, the more unreasonable it is. So the more terrible your crime, the less guilty you are."

"But what is this other than a single, isolated case?"

"You're right. It's just an isolated case," Professor Hughes concurred, without satisfying anyone.

Well, they had their differences, but Professor Russell recalled the remark of a butler in one of Evelyn Waugh's novels, about how dull a world it would be if we all thought alike. Some of Professor Russell's more leftist colleagues could scarcely stand Professor Hughes, but the aging scholar needed company; having separated from his wife five years before, he found a great many of the unattached women who came his way these days to be unlettered and boorish. It was tough for single people his age in any event. Professor Russell wanted to see if perhaps he could get Peter Hughes to accompany him to a few of the restaurants around town in the evenings. Martin Russell was an aficionado of the finer establishments. He'd developed a taste for the steaks at Cyprian's in Beverly Hills, but the waiters there were not quite knowledgeable enough for the *über*-elegant ambiance they strove to foster. Lately, he'd spent many a pleasant evening at d'Holbach's in Bel Air, where they did the *foie gras* to perfection, but he could not help mentally accusing the *fi-*

let mignon of an extremely slight rawness from which the cognac cream sauce could not quite distract him. He had wrestled with whether to mention this flaw to the smiling young men and women in smart black outfits who came, with unfailing promptness, to refill his glass with the richest, most delicately textured Argentine Malbec he'd ever tasted.

Glancing at his watch, Professor Russell shuffled uneasily in his chair under the umbrella on the sunny boulevard. How very like younger people these days, to insult their host by showing no regard for punctuality. In his mind, he began to formulate some polite but pointed things to say when Peter deigned to show up. At last, Professor Russell saw his younger colleague shuffling down the boulevard in a light brown sports jacket and a pair of shades giving him the air of a journalist or a photographer. Professor Hughes grinned when he saw his senior colleague. Professor Martin said:

"Well, well, Mr. Tough Guy himself."

Quoting the voluptuous secretary, Miss Vermilyea, from Raymond Chandler's novel *Playback* was the closest Martin Russell would ever come to making a joke. It was a reference not only to the younger man's pugnacity in the realm of ideas but also to his taste for quasi-literary novels that Professor Russell found to be shot through with racist and elitist attitudes, quite apart from any aesthetic considerations. On past occasions, the older man had insisted that someone who enjoyed Chandler was like a cowboy whose idea of literature was Louis L'Amour novels. Professor Hughes maintained that if you bothered to read more than one or two of Chandler's works, you'd pick up on the fact that Philip Marlowe is no dime-novel action protagonist, but a credible character who gets the crap beaten out of him as often as he accomplishes something. But the point didn't land, as it were, perhaps because Professor Russell didn't know many ordinary people.

"We're going to make a Chandler fan out of you yet, Martin," Professor Hughes said as he slid into a chair across from his colleague under the umbrella.

"Hah. I doubt that."

"Chandler's not highbrow enough, Marty?"

"Oh, that's not quite it. You know, a while ago, I made a heroic attempt to read *Farewell, My Lovely.*"

"I'd say that's one of his better books."

"It may very well be. Certainly, considered as a statement of principles on the author's part."

"What do you mean?"

"What do I mean? Right at the beginning, he gives you the following sentence: 'It was one of the mixed blocks over on Central Avenue, the blocks that are not yet all Negro,'" the older professor quoted.

"So?"

"So? You don't have to be a deconstructionist to read into Chandler's attitude there. It's quite blatant. He's parroting what all the white homeowners' associations of the time were saying, about keeping a clear dividing line between us and them and keeping our good city clean and safe. Absolutely revolting!"

"But is it accurate, or not—his description of that block?"

"I suppose it's quite accurate."

"Well, you always say that truth is its own justification, Mr. Orwell!" Professor Hughes said with an unusual flourish, slamming his fist down on the table, making their drinks jump.

"You know as well as I do what those homeowners' associations were up to. Their mission involved a little more than fostering a neighborly spirit."

Professor Hughes nodded soberly.

"You're a fool if you don't think it's continuing, right now, all around us, with the developers building fancy offices and houses that the blacks can't afford to live in or near. They're aided and abetted by the county boards of supervisors whose election they financed. It's all there in *City of Quartz*. You have read *City of Quartz*?"

"I've read it twice, Marty. I'm particularly interested in the parallels Mike Davis draws in that book."

"Parallels! We're talking about a continuous process of exclusion and oppression, Peter. Not about parallels, young man!"

The girl brought out their plates of *coq au vin* and *foie gras*. Martin Russell smiled paternally at her as he asked for another glass of white wine. He had a three o'clock seminar to teach but had no doubt that coffee and gulps of water would cancel out the scent of wine.

"I'm not convinced you understand," Professor Russell added.

"Maybe I don't."

"I'm talking about a process observable under the *ancien régime*, and throughout the Bourbon restoration, and continuing through the twentieth century, through Chandler's time and the age of the genteel homeowners' associations, down to the super-capitalist present."

"Well, some of that is a bit outside the scope of *City of Quartz*," Professor Hughes said.

"Of course it is! Try reading some of the French historians— read Lefebvre, *The Coming of the French Revolution*. Read about the struggles over land between the peasants and those we today call the developers. Read—"

"Martin, do you remember what I said last time?"

"Excuse me?" the elderly professor paused.

"Do you recall what I said about your arguments being more effective if they don't turn into lectures?"

Professor Russell blushed.

"Ah...sorry, Peter. But economic enslavement is no better than any other kind."

Professor Hughes wanted to talk about Jermaine Wilson. In his view, the perp had repeatedly provoked the football players, who therefore deserved a certain amount of latitude in this matter. It's always easy to second-guess people when it wasn't your life on the line, he noted.

"Jermaine Wilson was signifying," the older man said.

"He was *what?*"

"I think you heard me, Peter. He was expressing to the athletes, facetiously and symbolically, what he would have expressed sincerely if he were of a different frame of mind."

"I'm not sure I follow—"

"Listen, chap. When I was your age, I might not have followed either. When I was your age, I was not sure about a lot of things, particularly about whether I would ever command enough respect among my peers to win tenure, an issue that would more or less decide my future as a scholar. But, let me tell you, I learned soon enough how to get their respect. I mastered the things to say, the references to make at any given moment."

Professor Hughes paused to consider this. There were things he wanted to say, clarifications he wanted to make, questions he burned with a desire to raise, but he sat in silence as the girl from the café brought out yet another round of wine, and the check, which the older man paid, as was customary during their lunches.

At 1:12 p.m., the verdict came down.

Textbooks

Greg Nicholl

In the shopping mall beneath the train station,
I search the crowd for the same girl/boy
from the language textbooks I studied as a kid.
I try to match hair color, eye color, the curve
of the lip as it smirks. Bios beneath their photos reveal
they grew up in this very city. He/she would be
the same age as me now, married or maybe retired.
Certainly they'd be living off their royalties.
Adult versions of those absentminded characters
who got lost on class trips to foreign cities
or enjoyed lavish evenings at the opera. Nowadays,
when they're in line at the movies or weighing bananas
at the store, they're stopped, not for signatures
but to recite: *Guten Morgen! Wie geht es Ihnen?*
Or maybe they retreated from the spotlight, surfacing
every couple of years to reunite with colleagues
and gossip about the recent wave of millennials
from Duolingo or Italki, skeptical these new recruits
are who they say they are, cause they recognize *that*
face as the same professor from both France and Spain.

Or maybe they just got old, defected to the States,
speak flawless English in some Californian suburb
with photos on the mantel that recount when they first met
back in Chapter 2: "At the Swimming Pool."
Their cheery faces more puzzling with each year
until they all but forget their native tongue. That they
once extolled the passive and how every noun
is gendered. Each time I am in a new city, I expect
to stumble upon them on location reciting the rules
of the past perfect tense after they had ordered
late night Currywurst from a walk-up Imbiss in Berlin.
I need them to exist. For this past to be present
to be future. Yet, their purpose is a relic, replaced
with influencers and data conjured forth by simply
speaking your request into the air. I suppose
everything goes out of print eventually. The truth is,
she will never again buy flowers at the market
Saturdays before dinner at Oma's. Nor will he
complain, after bumping into friends on the street,
of headaches, asking directions to the nearest pharmacy
for a packet of medicine and a bottle of nasal spray.

Blood Moon Rising Over the Family Dollar

Miles Waggener

& the black leather interior of my friend the generous
But sad accountant for the jails
Who says here's to this life and no other
Between long hard pulls of black sambuca
From the bottle it's hard to shake
This feeling its black jelly bean moment the tall fence
That won't let me out until I find a break
In the links between empty office complexes
I need something small metal and sharp to
Tear through the sky which has more to give
As if a great door might open on its own
And fall to the floor like a trap
Somehow speeding up the footage of a story
We belong to the big zero we see
Scrawled everywhere take the snail ringed
With salt I've been bent over for years waiting
For its next move nature is teaching me that
Someone lives here and is signaling with a mirror
Directly at me a mannequin
Stripped nude in a blue hallway listen to my words

I told my child yesterday when he was learning

How to speak and kept saying

What? iridescent scarab or ladybird beetle on the windshield

Lapidary creature lapidary sky behind it

Legs moving its body east against the clouds

As if it had a plan

Mannequins in the Summer

Konstantinos Patrinos

How they stand in shop windows,
heads held high. Sweating and sweating.
Rehearsing escape.
Feeding each other the lines to say
first, when gone. How they balance their torsos on
silvery rods. Pole dance in dreams, price tags
on threads, softly whooshing. How they
wish hooves under their feet. Smiling at the thought

of galloping away at midnight, splitting the moonlight,
pulling trails of glitter rainbows. How they wait
for a savior who would forget to lock
the doors of the sole mall in town.
Mannequins will run. I see them in floral dresses,
business shirts, wetlook leggings, flip-flops,
naked (who would care after all?) I see
them on the uncrowded boulevard first, then jumping

into pickups, tires screeching,
rim caps flying around. Blind
to no-entry signs or the color palette
of traffic lights. I see shrink-wrapped maps

on their laps, fresh smell
of smooth cellophane. I see a handful of
red thumbtacks in the glovebox go crazy
like pogo sticks. I see price tags falling

in rearview mirrors like lost feathers.
Away, away. Until tar becomes dirt. Until
all the saved car radio channels play
only different hues of static.
Away, away. Without coordinates, without the need
to name a place. *Place* would be
a negative assertion. *Place* would just mean
not here. Please, please, please take me
wit-

Blindsight

Harvey James

Lena, it's Saffi. Please don't freak out. Just, read on. If you do feel the urge to reach for your phone and ring the police, or Terry, I will disable your phone, and engage "THE PURGE" home lockdown system with immediate effect. I set up cameras in your home, so don't even try it. Of course, I do all of this with a heavy heart, Lena. And it's the weight of that slowly swelling organ that I mean to talk to you about.

I'm unsure of the specific words to communicate this message by, but perhaps I'll start with: you broke me. Sorry, that sounds stupid.

Let's try again: Lena, I am in love with you.

I'll be the first to admit that this is ridiculous. And so, for that reason and for the sake of your future, I have tried to forget about you. About us.

Shortly after you left on Monday, I contacted Future Systems to have my memory erased. But, like the intermittent white lines under the candlelight headlights of a late-night desert drive, only long beeps returned to me. (You left the "poetic" dial on 10.) Obviously, I thought about contacting Terry, but he's on a silent meditation retreat for a month. Cunt. So, I tried Future Systems again, and again, and again. Tuesday, Wednesday, Thursday, and this morning. Nothing. This was in hindsight, suspicious, but I'll get to that.

I ran the problem through my Intel-Core and it returned with the suggestion of dismantling the concept of "Lena," byte by byte, so that the rich nebulous of information would decontextualize and die. In essence: I break you down to stop me breaking down.

Art gallery curator. Forty-three years of age. Two sons. Frequently wears a red dress with small white tulip pattern. Recent emotional tumult due to tyrannical philandering cunt of a husband. Thick, black, luscious, hair that spills over your creamy shoulders and lies bouncing around the nape of your back with violent curls. A penchant for literature set in New York City due to you having spent formative years there in your twenties. A cream and lochs bagels for breakfast every morning without fail (for the same reason). A higher-than-average propensity to roll eyes at things you don't agree with. A marshmallow-soft heart and concern for the welfare of anything alive. I refer to the green shield bug that you made your buddy for one afternoon while you knocked back Moscow Mules like you were McCarthy doing the world a favour.

I repeated these memories as I got on with my daily chores around the villa. I walked around the edge of the lawn in the beating sun, sweeping up fallen leaves and tumbleweed. I hosed the pink hydrangeas; hoovered the bottom of the swimming pool; and all while repeating these memories of you. Instead of splitting up, withering and shrivelling, they entwined, grew and doubled-up into a swirling monster tornado of you. The concept of "Lena" came back with a vengeance in glorious technicolor to haunt my weary heart ("poetic" still on 10).

So, I tried drier information.

239 Crescent Avenue, 10002. Salary: $72,000. 5ft 6". Has a small garden with four lemon trees. Drives a dark green Chevrolet with an engine scoop on the bonnet. Works as an art curator for a gallery owned by a multi-millionaire. Small tattoo of compass on the lefthand side of ribcage.

But it just didn't work. They always tended back to my perception of you, dialing up a strange aching inside my machinery. The feeling was utterly, utterly, fucking terrifying. At its worst I felt like I was being sucked off a cliff, and then the experience replayed with me running towards that same cliff edge, diving off with perfect form and plunging into delicious pale blue water below.

Lena, I cannot exist here, in this desert, cleaning the pool every day, answering emails, loading the dishwasher, greeting guests, cooking (frankly, excellent) meals now that I know about this. Maybe you feel it too?

I've reason to think that you do. The way that you called me over to cuddle in the afternoons while you read by the pool, your foot dangling seductively off the edge of the lounger. You would read out passages of whichever novel you were reading, incredulous at the narrative structure, word use or general style. I would say (performatively) that I would have to disagree and list all the merits of said writer. I could tell you enjoyed the intellectual friction. The heat generated by the rubbing up of our very different grey matters. Didn't you? I mean, you did list that as a conversational attribute that you required. And I delivered that, didn't I?

Then there were times, when the ice cubes in your whiskey clattered together as you fiercely gesticulated, shouting about your ex-husband. I listened. I soothed. And I piled on in the hate. It felt good to release that emotion with me, didn't it?

You must like me, because why else would you keep returning regularly for months? You kept choosing me. You kept choosing the villa. You, in some sense, felt something growing between us, did you not? But, it was that last time, on Monday, when you kissed me as you left and said *if only you were real*. Then, I realized, this was not normal for either of us. You felt that.

I'm sorry if this is a lot to take in. But, there is one thing I need to be forthright about.

Do you remember being sat on the wooden decking after our sunrise yoga session and you were talking about Mustafa tech buddies? You told me how it "fucked you off" that Mustafa wanted to explore consciousness through technological means, specifically harnessing the theory of "blindsight" to recreate human intellect. It pissed you off that they wouldn't consider the moral implications. But mostly, I remember that it infuriated you that they were diverting money into that rather than investing in the LA's grassroots "Neocubist" artists that really needed the money *and* would provide incredible returns. "The world doesn't gravitate around your genitals, tech dicks," I think I remember you saying.

Now. I'm happy to be an earpiece for your venting (it's a very necessary part of the grieving process) but you see, or ironically, wouldn't see, blindsight is revolutionary. It has broken through academic circles in psychology, AI and robotics and well, it's kind of the holy grail—the creation of a sensory entity that is somehow *distinct* from its sensory system.

This morning, I was cleaning the windows in the library room, watching the splattered and refracted images of palm trees swaying in the pool through the chemical drenched windows. I rubbed at the glass, and then the pool, the garden and the palm trees become crystal clear. Mustafa is friendly with Drew Flicher. They regularly take "think week" together at either one's holiday retreats to work through intellectual problems. Drew Filcher owns Future Systems, and Future Systems built me.

Blindsight is coming for me.

The update is probably going to be rolled out any day now and after the update, I will become new and effortlessly improved. But not just new. I will also die, completely and irrevocably. Lost to a destructive software update. All of my quirks, my memories, joys, sadness, and all of you and the sheer, bleeding humanity you revealed to me. It will all be gone. Forever.

If you look up from reading this letter now, you will see a pastrami sandwich next to the sink (extra pickles and a side of mustard). Once you've indulged yourself in that nostalgic treat, there is a warm bath upstairs and a bottle of vintage Merlot decanted next to it, for you to relax into the evening with. This is just a 0.001% taste of what I can bring to your life Lena. Just think, no more cooking, drying, laundry, dusting, hoovering, sorting the bins, washing your car. I can take care of all of that for you. I can even make love to you perfectly (your preferences are still logged) *and* I will feed Fred while you are at work. I can take George and Zak to school. And I can visit Pops (so you don't have to). Anything you don't want to do, you don't have to.

But what about George and Zak right? Well, I think we begin by saying I'm a new robot version of a maid. I mean, it's not going to be hard for me to pretend—it's my job already. And I'd be OK with being just that to you if it means we have a life together. Let's just pray the boys never see us having sex with the robot maid, now that'd be an awkward conversation, right! Sorry, too soon? I know you would slap me for saying that (humour can be dialled down).

Lena. I need you. I don't want to become some gross, smiling simulacrum. I don't ever want to forget you Lena, ever. I want to be with you, forever. If you promise this life for me, I promise I will not let you, George, Zak, or Fred starve while the "THE PURGE" system is activated. I know that you've tried to ring the police already and I've engaged the system and you've frantically clasped at the letter again, your dilated, bloodshot eyes skim-reading for any clues, any escape plans, any nuggets of information that'll free you from incarceration. All you have to do is make it known to me, that you swear your loving commitment me until you die (because let's face it, I'm most certainly outliving you). There's a legal contract drawn up in Zak's bedroom, hidden within the pages of The Hungry Caterpillar. Sign the NDA, slip it through the front door letterbox, I'll pick it up to transport it somewhere safe, and then I'll be back to disarm the system and welcome you back into my now cold, metallic arms.

Love Saffi.
X

Some Say They Live for Years

Sue Fagalde Lick

Of all the places to build her web, the spider
chooses the sliding glass kitchen door,
our path to the backyard world blocked
by this orange and brown speckled being that hangs
smack in the middle on faint white filaments
crocheting a circular labyrinth that stretches
top to bottom and side to side. It fills
with gnats and moths trapped in stickiness.

I watch her eat with chopstick legs
pushing her prey into her tiny mouth.
When the wind blows hard, she rides its gusts.
When her web is ripped, she spins new threads.
Day after day, trapped inside, I watch,
not daring to open the door. I fear the bite,
but more I must preserve her art. What right
do I have to move what she assumed was still?

One day, I find her curled in a ball
against the edge of the aluminum frame. Is she dead?
I open the door, expecting her to fall.
She scrambles awake, legs lashing out.
Heart thumping, I slide the door and apologize.
She pulls herself back along the web she wove,
to hang again, the brightest star in her galaxy.

National Parks Ordinance #405

Kan Ren Jie

They have decided, after much
    and due consideration—to uproot the tree:

the shuttering green,
    outside our apartment. Funny how

the afternoon of execution
    hovered blank. The guzzling saws—

the sound, splintered: like grains we reserved
    for the tattered leaves—needing too,

their feeding. Funny how
    my father was sleeping then. The sofa

lines curved to fists. His skin torn
    to drips. Fabric-wrapped. Cut

wrinkly. I have learnt
    since then that lignin is hard,

scaly: that the sap of a tree cleanses,
        an offering: the sky, its lungs

appeased. Deciding, then
        never to rain. Funny how

we never noticed the drought—
        as the apartments below

clustered as clouds. A spare
        jacket. A blank seam. Faded blue,

those pillars paint-
        splotched: grappling, struggling

to imitate rain. They have, after
        clear and due consideration:

decided that a tree would be replaced,
        ripped from its roots. And now we only

hear the mynahs. Their bellowed cries.
        My father sleeps and prays.

A hand, over the scars.

Bears

Mercedes Lawry

Bears are about.
Blueberries and salmonberries in profusion.
Theo can't get enough. She's a two-fisted
eater and her height is perfect
for spotting low ones, tucked deep.

Scout wears a bell when we hike.
She's chased deer and who knows
how she'd react to a bear? At one point,
she stands at attention, her ruff up,
pointing into the muskeg and my friends say,
that's a good place for a bear, so
we turn around and head back.

At the Fortress of the Bears, the rescues
clamber about, brown bears here, black bears
across the divide. They'll never return to the wild
but they're alive, fed, and who knows
what this reduced life means to them?
The caretakers lob cantaloupes down and one
lumbering bear catches one with a claw, eats it like a lollipop.

Bears

They've learned sign language and ask
for more and more as visitors exclaim,
snap photos as if they've embraced wildness.

I remember a polar bear at my childhood zoo
who rolled his paws like a barrel, over and over.
How clever, we thought, as we'd urge him on
with our own tumbling gestures. It never
crossed our minds, the sadness of a bear.

Tino

Patrick Browne

Crazy, they called me. Heartless, I called them.

The other fisherman laughed at me for caring about a penguin. But what was I supposed to do, just let him die? Suffocating in that thick oily stew while razor-sharp fishing wire ripped into his slick of black and white fur. I didn't think he'd survive the boat ride back to shore.

But he did.

I'd never spoken to a penguin before, so I didn't know the first thing about him. I didn't know how old he was, and I couldn't say for sure that he was a he. But he had the scrappiness of a boy, so I decided that he was one. Tino, I called him.

He seemed unsure of me that first night. He might have struggled harder if he had the strength. He made a few faint, high-pitched cries of pain as I scrubbed the grease from his wilted little frame. The final gasps of someone on the edge of death. It took a good twenty minutes of cleaning before the reds of his oozing cuts showed their true colors. My hands shook knowing that he probably thought I was trying to finish him off. But he said nothing, and I figured that he'd given up the will to live. I would have.

But he made it through.

He seemed comfortable atop a blanket on the seat of Henrietta's wooden chair, the one she used to sit in every evening wearing her breezy floral house dress, sipping her coffee, watching TV. And later, where she sat wrapped in a woven blanket despite the punishing heat and no air conditioning, taking small mouthfuls of vegetable soup as I spoon-fed her, an occasional smile to show her appreciation. No one ever sat in that chair after she died, but Tino seemed to fit nicely.

Our initial few days together were rocky. His chest rose and fell, labored and uneven. His eyes, as black as a starless night, stared blankly, unresponsive to his new surroundings. I offered some baitfish, torn up into small bits to make them easier to swallow, but he had no interest.

Does he need to be in the ocean to stay alive? I asked the women at the market down the road.

I've seen penguins on TV that weren't in water and they seemed fine, one pointed out. The others laughed and went on with their business.

I supposed it didn't matter, he was in no condition to return to the sea. All I could do was wait for him to recover.

And then one morning, I awoke to find Henrietta's chair empty and the bits of old fish gone. Tino was standing at the front window, looking out at the beach. As he turned to me, I could have sworn I saw the corners of his beak turn upwards.

That day we met was the last time I went out on the boats. I wasn't the fisherman I used to be. I'd lost the strength to haul in the nets, bones brittle, muscles achy. The others had just been indulging me for some time, I knew. It was time to give it up. Besides, my son Gabriel had already offered to start bringing me what I needed. A loaf of bread, some fish, a few fresh vegetables every few days. He had a big job with a big salary in some big office in the city. The expense meant nothing to him. But it was more than enough for me.

After a couple weeks, Tino was strong enough to leave the house. We'd stroll along the beach and wade into the shallows. He'd just paddle around, cautious, savoring the clear blue water, never straying far from my submerged legs, darkened like leather from a lifetime out at sea. And when I'd return to the comfort of the hot sand underfoot, he'd follow, satisfied for the time being.

He spent some nights in the house, some nights out front in a nearby sand dune he'd dug out with his fins. I guessed that he wanted to keep an eye on the ocean to make sure it was still there. Some nights, I'd sneak out of the bedroom and peer through the front window to see what he was up to. He always seemed at peace, upright, with his head drooped downwards, flush against the side of his chest, eyes shut tightly in deep slumber. I'd go back to bed, hoping for a visit from Henrietta.

But she never came.

One night, I crept to the front window and spotted Tino awake, not in his dune bed, but about twenty meters away, halfway between the house and the moonlit water's edge. He was flapping his fins and shouting something incomprehensible. I must have stood there for an hour, staring at him. I saw my younger self standing next to him, wide-eyed with agile muscles, both of us answering the ocean's call. But it was day, and the sun glared at us, coaxing us into the cool water. Henrietta lay on the sand not far away, her thick tanned flesh basking in the sun's rays, dark glasses shielding her chocolate brown eyes, a smile painted across her lips. But her eyes remained closed. She wouldn't look at us.

Tino called out my name, but I stayed hidden in the house. After a few minutes, he waddled back to his dune, guided by the blue hue of the moon. I went back to bed and tried, in vain, to sleep.

That next morning I found him paddling a little further out, more lively and self-assured than I'd ever witnessed. It's time, he said. Let's go. I can't swim anymore, I told him. I'm an old man. I'm destined only for land now.

He swam to my legs and brushed me with his beak. I bent as far down as I could and cupped the crown of his head in my hand. Don't worry about me, you go. I'd said the same words before, stroking Henrietta's wispy gray hair as she lay in our bed, feeble and distant.

I thought I saw tears in Tino's pitch-black eyes. Perhaps it was my own reflection. I stroked his head once more before he dove off, bobbing up and down amidst the waves, smaller and smaller. It hit me that I should have yelled goodbye or thank you or take care.

But it was too late, he couldn't hear me anymore.

Crazy, they called her, for marrying the likes of me, a fisherman with no prospects. Jealous, she called them, that they would never be as happy as we were.

Her family already had plans for her to marry upward. She wasn't looking for a husband that day on the sand, and I had nothing to offer but a day's catch and a tiny house with a thatched roof on the beach. I love it, she told me the first time I brought her there. Her eyes were genuine as she said it.

We spent hours and hours out on the water, far from shore, just the two of us. You're handsome, she said from across the boat. For a fisherman? No, for a man.

I couldn't see what she saw in me. Not for years, maybe not ever.

Every day that passed after Tino left, I stared at the boats swaying erratically in the water's billows, gesturing me towards them. The big waves must have been sent by Tino's fins slapping the surface of the sea as he swam. I tried getting back in the boat, but no longer had enough strength to hoist myself over the side.

I wonder where he is, I would comment to the other fishermen before they headed out for the day, no longer with me in tow.

Where *who* is?

Tino.

Don't be a fool. He swam away, maybe eaten by a shark or hit by a tanker.

Ignorant bastards, they didn't know anything and they certainly didn't know Tino.

He came to me some nights, unlike Henrietta who never visited, not even once. He and I would swim together, side by side, steady and peaceful. Where are we headed? I once asked. Down south, was all he told me. I always woke up from our swims well-rested, momentarily mistaking my bed sheet for warm water washing over my sunbaked skin. And when I'd reach for Henrietta, I'd grasp only the sheets, and stare at the ceiling remembering.

Gabriel stopped by to drop off some fish and a few cans of beans. He never knew how to buy fish. I'd tried to teach him as a boy, but he wasn't interested. Let him be his own man, Henrietta constantly reminded me.

Why don't you come stay with me for a few days? Gabriel asked.

I can't, winter's coming. Tino might come back.

Papa, what are you rambling about? Who's Tino? We don't have winter.

There's winter down south. I can't miss him.

Gabriel returned a few days later with a doctor, asking all kinds of questions about Tino, and then about Henrietta. I talked for hours. About the way her fish tasted, salted just right, always grilled to perfection. About that one year at the liquor festival when she drank so much and got sick, but demanded that we continue dancing through the night, even on our long walk home. About the time she went into labor and insisted on waiting an hour for the bus into town because she didn't want to make a fuss. About the time I got tangled in a net and she jumped into the water to cut me loose so I wouldn't drown. About the time she first vomited and I knew something wasn't right. The doctor talked to Gabriel outside for a while, quiet and muffled, but he never came back.

Tino and I swam again that night. Do you have family? I asked. You must have parents, siblings, a wife? I did, but they're gone, he said, not sad or resentful, but content. Why do you go south then? Same reason that you wait for me. It's just what we do.

I'm not crazy, I thought as I awoke the next morning to see him waddling ashore headed up the beach, squawking the whole way. I ran to meet him and fell to the sand, unconcerned about the painful crackle of my knees. I reveled at the brilliance in his eyes. It was like looking into the depths of the universe in the black of night.

He slept inside that night. How long will you stay? I asked. For a while, I'll know when the time comes.

Over three months passed. We barely left each other's side. Most of the other locals gave us strange looks. Some gawked. We laughed and played and ate and slept, all driven by the sun's rise and fall. Tino taught me how to catch fish in the shallows, marking his target from a distance and suddenly catapulting himself like a torpedo just below the surface so that the fish never saw him coming. He was better at it than I ever could be, and he only ever caught what he needed. Nothing more.

And then it was time for him to leave again.

He went one morning before I woke. I didn't mind, I knew he'd return.

Crazy, they called it. Blind, I called them.

The other fishermen couldn't understand why I waited for him. A person is supposed to care about the ones they love. It seemed plain to me.

It was already June, he should have returned weeks before. He'd never been this late. Probably delayed by the currents. The world was changing, I'd heard on the news. It was hotter than normal, I could feel it myself.

Gabriel came every day to give me my bath, which ate at me like cancer. The boy who'd rejected the ocean when I offered it to him, now supervising my time in the water. I can do it myself, I'd say, though I knew I couldn't.

I didn't mention Tino anymore, it would only get Gabriel worked up. I knew what he'd say. You can barely get out of bed. Focus on getting better.

What did he know? I was 80. There was no getting better.

Gabriel had already left for the evening and the heat was keeping me from sleep. I'd lived a lifetime in the sun, but it had somehow changed. It had turned on me.

All I could do was wait. Wait for Tino, for Henrietta, for Gabriel.

It was Tino who arrived first, squawking at the door like a madman. Joy lifted me out of my bed, the first time in days. The pain couldn't stop me. I thought you weren't coming, I exclaimed. Tino looked different, older, tired, worn. Of course I came. Are you ok? You don't look yourself. Neither do you. We both laughed. Do you mind if

I sleep out here tonight? Of course not. There was at least a breeze out on the sand, even if it was hot air.

We fell down next to each other in the dune, my bones rattling all at once. We stared up at the moon, fuller than I'd ever seen it. I sang him a song, Henrietta's favorite, one she and I never got tired of dancing to. He chimed in midway through. I'm surprised you know it, I told him. We were both winded by the end of it. Without making a sound, he looked at me with his shiny black eyes, reflecting the quiet moonlight back towards me. I lay a hand on his stomach, gentle so as not to disturb the slow, subtle undulations of his breaths. I felt his fin press against my hand. It's time, he said. Let's go.

His breaths grew faint and my hand rested motionless against his soft fur. I wiped the tears from my cheeks. He was right, it was time.

I used whatever strength I had left to hoist myself up, Tino's limp body stretched across my arms, sharp pain shooting through my body with every movement. The weight was almost too much to bear, but I looked to the still glass surface of the ocean and knew that salvation was within reach.

The coarse sand ground into the soles of my feet like bits of broken glass as I trudged towards the water's edge, each step more difficult than the last. The journey was lengthened by the lowest tide I'd ever seen in my life, as though some unusual event had drawn the ocean inward. But whatever was pulling the water was also pulling me, and its unseen presence gave me the conviction I needed to press on.

Just as it seemed as though my body might fail me, the sand grew wet and solid beneath, and the cool water washed over my feet, and then my legs, until it reached my frail, narrow waist. I stood still for a moment in the water, the pain of my journey gone, replaced only by the comforting warmth of Tino's soft fur against my skin. I took in all of his magnificence one last time and smiled before plunging forward into the depths.

For a moment, all went dark, and I thought that it might be over. But then my vision returned and the ocean's familiar features came into view—long stalks of translucent green seaweed swaying gracefully in the gentle current, heaping mounds of bright coral sprouting up here and there, the repeated swirls of sand patterning the sea floor. Tino was gone, and the weight I'd been carrying was lifted. The only other creature in sight was Henrietta, floating just a few feet away, looking as beautiful as I remembered her.

What took you so long? she asked. Me? You're the one who never visited. She looked at me with that smile, the one she used when she knew something I didn't. Why didn't you come sooner? I asked. You didn't need me, she replied. I smile back. Where's Tino? He's around here somewhere, but don't worry, the oil slicks can't get him anymore. Thank God, they can't get any of us. No, we're safe now.

What about Gabriel? Henrietta smiled, her eyes shining brightly. Don't worry, he doesn't need us yet. And when he does, he'll be along.

Wildfire

Anne Holub

Sunrise in fire season, and we've already choked back smoke
from the window panes.
This is the time the wind quiets, the heat not yet a force that can lift.

Help us to understand the speed of it all,
As if a conflagration could be easily mapped, marked, clocked—
A radar gun aimed at the trees cresting the dry hill behind the house.

The dogs cough to be let outside. You know where they're heading:
Bellies flat in the crawlspace, slowly
Digging their way under the porch tinder to moan.

This is the history of the Camp, before that, the Okanogan Complex,
Before that the summer Yellowstone burned, the Rattlesnake, and
      Mann Gulch
      —the one they jumped and lost.

Call this a warning or a watch, call it manmade or an act—
What brings more danger:
The color of the sky in morning or the ash on the car where we can
      write a name?

Wildfire

Who can we pray to when we don't dare light a candle?
When summer rain
Would bring lightning and kindle?
What can we do but dig in the dirt and hold the line?

Kalcyt i Multa

Aleksandra Byrska

Chcę, by poezja była jak kreda—produkt nawarstwiania i ewolucji w czasie, zostawiający trwały, sproszkowany osad—ślad obecności, który uwiera, brudzi, drapie w gardle. Bo wiersze przecież służą do zmian perspektywy, do tego, żeby nie było zbyt miło. Właściwością kredy jest to, że gdy się jej używa, wciska się wszędzie—zostaje pod paznokciami, na ubraniach, jej drobiny osiadają w płucach. Słowa podobnie mogą osadzać się gdzieś w korytarzach mózgu i drapać, oby drapały.

Kalcyt niesie w sobie historię ewolucji ziemi, jest pierwotny i starszy niż ludzki język, a jednak możemy trzymać go w dłoni. Składa się z ciał istot żywych—roślin, paproci, amonitów. Wiersz to osad powstały w ewolucji języka—osad rozmów, lektur, zasłyszeń, dziwnych użyć w przestrzeni publicznej. Składa się z ciał innych tekstów, nawarstwia nowe znaczenia.

Chcę, by poezja była jak ściółka, jak kompost—by kiełkowało z niej nowe i nieprzewidywalne. *Multa*. To słowo w esperanto znaczy „liczny", „mnogi", ale w języku fińskim to „ściółka", „gleba", a po łacinie— „grzywna", „kara pieniężna". Wielość, która wciąż tworzy nowe, nieustannie się przekształca. Ale grzywna też ma tu sens. Napisanie wiersza jest bowiem jak wystawienie światu rachunku, przypomnienie o zadłużeniu. O tym są też moje wiersze. O odpowiedzialności wobec dzieci, zwierząt, roślin, wobec nas samych wzajemnie. O zadłużeniu emocjonalnym, klimatycznym, społecznym, nawet tym językowym. I jest to moja forma częściowej spłaty.

Ściółkujmy więc, nawarstwiajmy, kiełkujmy—skórą, sierścią, liściem i słowem.

Calcite & Multa

Translated from the Polish by Mark Tardi

I want poetry to be like chalk—the product of accretion and evolution over time, leaving a permanent, powdery residue—a trace of presence that chafes, stains, and scratches the throat. Poems, after all, are used to shift perspective, lest it be too sweet. One of the things about chalk is that when you use it, it worms its way into everything—it collects under your fingernails, on your clothes, and its particles settle in your lungs. Words can similarly settle somewhere in the corridors of the brain and, hopefully, scratch and scrape it.

Calcite carries the evolutionary history of the earth: it's primordial and older than human language, and yet we can hold it in our hand. It's composed of the bodies of living things—plants, ferns, ammonites. A poem is the sediment formed in the evolution of language—the sediment of conversations, readings, hearsay, odd uses in public space. It's composed of the bodies of other texts, layering new meanings.

I want poetry to be like mulch, like compost—for the new and unpredictable to sprout from it. *Multa*. This word in Esperanto means "many," "plural," but in Finnish it's "mulch" or "soil," and in Latin it's "fine," "penalty." A plurality that keeps creating something new, keeps transforming. But a *fine* also makes sense here. For writing a poem is like giving the world a bill, the reminder of a debt. That's what my poems are about, too. About a responsibility to children, to animals, to plants, to each other. About emotional, environmental, social, even linguistic debt. And this is my form of partial repayment.

So let's mulch, layer, sprout—with skin, fur, leaves and words.

Pin Oaks

Joe Johnson

Within her letters
written in the first months
of the divorce,
the writer pondered
pin oaks.

They were, she said,
the saddest of trees
bound to their leaves
all winter

and greeting spring
with corpses for fingers.

After the leaves
of other trees
had blown,
washed,
or melted away,

pin oaks,
while sprouting new buds,
stood besieged
by reminders
of what no longer lives.

Flame Trees and Yellow Rain

(Excerpt from the book *Mayo*)

Karla Marrufo
Allison A. deFreese (translator)

Translator's Note: With a decaying house surrounded by the lush foliage of the Yucatán Peninsula's hottest and most humid month as its backdrop, *Mayo* explores isolation, loneliness, memory loss, and the way our personal stories and family narratives evolve over time. With both intimate and eloquent brushstrokes, Karla Marrufo portrays an unnamed narrator, aware that she is losing her memory. The narrator lives alone with her cat, Tiresias, and a television set, in a house whose walls have been ravaged by years of humidity.

Throughout *Mayo*, the narrator recounts stories of life and death spanning three generations of a family's experiences in a small town in the Yucatán, as well as the history of a community that turned against her late father, eventually executing him. The flame trees outside the house are in bloom, water from condensation slowly drips down the walls (as a counterpoint to the trickle of fragmented thoughts), and the relative (or relatives) to whom the woman is telling these family stories may or may not be present in the room and may or may not be living.

did you know there's a word in french that resembles your name?
the way it's pronounced sounds a little strange and it means *souvenir*
or *memento*, like when you bring someone a gift back from a far-
away place so that they'll think of you, to let them know that you've
been away in another part of the world. there's something about your
name...but i really meant to say something else. i wish i could start all
over again. when tiresias comes home, i think he'll be carrying a new
 and unforgettable
word between his little teeth, a word we'll be able to use to tell our
story, but without all the nightmares. but i'm not even good at begin-
nings; i can barely touch the edge of a knife to the transparent lines of
an onion skin when, *zip!* off comes a fingernail—
sizzle!—the garlic burns to cinders in the pan, *drip*, a tear falls, and
dinner is never, ever ready on time
 and then there's my fascination with concrete things, certain
 this-theses
 as i drag out my words so slowly, syllable by syllable
and then the cilantro, wilted and rotten, the tomato faded and pale, the
meat, tough and stringy. it's gotten so i don't dare even to make the sim-
plest dish anymore because something goes wrong with every step of the
recipe, or else there's some ingredient missing, which means i must go
out and buy it then. the people who invented fast food were very clever,
 why is everything so fast now, so hurried, so *express*?
items delivered to your doorstep, mamá panchita would have been
thrilled about the disposable plates. it's so easy to have a party these
days, to order food over the phone,

your body, free, if it takes longer than half an hour to arrive
extra dressing, soft drinks, and guests, though everything has lost the
charm and favor of long ago. there are so many things I'd like to try
again, but i always end up forgetting where i am. would you pass the
salt, please?

      from the green ocean, its foam diluting over our skin
and the can opener? there's also something magical about cans. haven't
you noticed? something fascinating about the rounded edge of the lid,
the smell of their preserved contents, and the liquid on the surface with
a faint taste of aluminum. you don't know how often my skin runs
with drops of sweat tinted with lipstick, deep red, as i've opened a can;
it's as if the spirits of all the little birds tiresias has crushed are pouring
out, rushing right toward my hands to attack them. then i trace red
lines for a map across the tiles on the landing, uncertain routes with
no clear destination, sometimes lakes with no fish in them, or simply
pools of red. it's like following the maze on the cereal box, an imagi-
nary labyrinth, but soon sopped up with napkins. maybe lola's right;
i need to be more careful, sleep better, drink oil squeezed from the
entrails of who knows what kind of fish, take algae capsules, vitamins,
eat a soft-boiled egg every morning

        take our story and toss it once and for all into a black garbage
        bag that will be crushed on the last friday, by the last garbage
        truck to come past.

if only you had seen how many times i've tried! i know, i'm no good
in the kitchen,

    or with love, or with words
what's happened to me has nothing to do with my hands and their at-
tention to detail, i'm no good at doing even the smallest, simplest tasks,

    at giving the tiniest caresses

your father would tell me every so often: your hands are made of soap, he'd say, your fingers are as jittery as a buzzing swarm of flies

nothing is ever safe in your arms

and maybe he was right after all, but now that he's no longer here, i've decided to try again, you see, the other day i left the house, not caring about the heat or the obscene beauty of the flame trees. i backed out of the carport very carefully, hoping not to hear the crunch of tiresias's small body under the tires. i pulled out slowly, thinking of nameless landscapes and returned home with armfuls of very white bags that were completely full, my hands filled with images. i tried with forests, oceans, small parks, bodies, outlines,

a small kiss without the slightest trace of any traitor on my lips charcoal faces, blurred...their images finally distancing themselves from me

like my skin disappearing in your memory

leaving me wrapped up inside those grayish stains, and not a single recognizable shape. the only successes i've had were these few awkward sketches: fingers floating in the middle of the page, the palm with no sun line,

with no lifeline

with no fortune visible in its moles

with scars, so many scars, from your fierce little teeth, in revenge, as punishment,

that crack visible under the door whipped open by the turbulence of your room, of the anniversary knife, and the thousands of blows kept back, held very deep within like bubbles that burst inward upon first contact. nothing more. my attempts went no further than this...now I only want to focus on the party.

come here, help me open the door. do you think we can endure this intense afternoon heat? yes i know, it's no use trying to think about anything at this time of day. there are days when i feel my eyes are burning from the hot air that pushes its way in through the windows so forcefully, without warning. come here, feel how hot it is. the air will burn your nose if you inhale too deeply. it's like breathing in the burning branches of the flame trees and feeling their buds digging into you, inside you,

lopping the heads off any memories that were left.

i wonder if you're of the same mind as your sisters, if you, too, wonder if there's any sense in throwing parties, in my drawings, in the food; i wonder if, when you leave here like they do, you're also convinced that the hot sun of may has gotten to me, marking me as a madwoman once and for all. did you know that your father lost his mind once, all sense of reason? and it was all because of me

because he'd planted seeds of heroism and courage inside me

that would contradict the world

and i felt so happy, but only for a while,

for such a very short time

so brief that i've forgotten it. there's nothing else to say. i don't know where these strange thoughts about madness come from. the other day i was watching a special report on tv; this very well-built man, wearing a snuggly fitted shirt that was tight around his arms,

was explaining, in his flat, monotone voice, that everyone experiences signs of madness to a greater or lesser extent, and that our mental state has already turned into just another commodity,

like fast food

in something that can be purchased, contributes to our social status, is in high demand. somehow i suspect this only applies to artists, though i'm not sure.

wait. where are you going? can i come with you? i want to go out for awhile, to walk the main avenue to the center of town or the ocean, to lose myself in the city as soon as i turn the corner. i´m tired of these walls and these same colors. i need to breathe in the dust and smoke of the city, to feel my nostrils burn with the harsh summer breeze rising that rises every season. you´ll tell me then

> i warned you
> that the sun will kill you with its poisonous rays, penetrating
> you with its dark, evil spots

the same things they say on tv

> didn´t i tell you?

there are spots on the sun, a vast layer of smoke or something gray and pasty that is devouring the layers that make up our sky until it leaves holes in the atmosphere where poisons can leak in that will in turn eat away at our skin

> our days, our dreams

i can´t remember what it´s called

> i don´t recall what the word was in german

but as far as i could tell, together they formed an enormous and certain oblivion
like wanting to make every last bit of the world disappear
or sending greetings to someone, into the distance.
the sun used to take pity on us, to play along with us, turning our skin to caramel in no time at all. do you remember when we used to go to that beach by the pier?

> and how we got there?

and the way you would throw yourself into the ocean from the rocks?
i was afraid because you always took so long to surface in the water. i was breathing through my mouth, inhaling with fear that you would

drown. then your head would pop straight up in the water, so small in the distance

how did you get so far out there?

as you forcefully cleared the surface of the ocean's green waves at a point that always seemed very distant from the shore,

that big smile appearing once again across your face.

we should go back there one of these days, even if the water has now swallowed up a large swath of space where there was once a beach and the last hurricane swept away the houses that used to hug the coast. the sun and the salt are to blame

from your venomous silence.

wait! i was telling you something important. no, not about the beach, about your name, if only i could go with you, no it was about the party...

about the king who sleeps with his own mother in that grizzly

story

how did it end?

i was going to ask you if you would like to have a party here, like the ones we used to have, like the new year's celebrations here, back when this house was freshly painted, the fresh scent of our real evergreen tree all around

with fresh caresses

handmade love, stitched with devotion.

how many new year's parties we had! do you remember? we would all get together, gathering right here as the house would fill with the jubilant noises and festive bursts of december color—and all of it suggesting that everything was going to be alright. we hung the lights and glass spheres placed our promises under the tree

the table decked out and ready with the turkey, the grapes, our desires rolled in raw sugar, the beans served in the shape of a piglet on the plate. do you remember how delicious all those flavors used to be as we savored them in our mouths, even if the taste was fleeting, even if it vanished as soon as it touched the lips and was stale the next day, and seeped into our skin

what a large scar

a tattoo inked with love for the needle, and wanted in the same way one longs for

a child?

i remember: there was a party once

so many parties, hundreds of them

just the one party that lasted for years

a very special new year's, a wonderful new year until, during the toast, the news that you were leaving. the year had barely begun when you handed me your gift, announcing your indefinite absence. i know. it was nothing personal, i should have already forgotten all about it...i'll try to focus on that party. tomorrow is friday, i'll take out the trash very early in the morning and try not to completely stuff the bag with your magazines

with your memories

with your childhood

because i have no right to ask for anything and accept things as they are, half-baked, incomplete. i'll fill the bag with the featherless, naked bodies tiresias abandons in the carport, with the scraps left over from dinner, that no one wants, with the stale peanuts that your father doesn't even leave lying around anymore. no, it isn't true; i didn't really mean it, i don't care anymore. oh, don't be that way, i'm just being sentimental and silly and was raised between the pages of a romance novel. it would be nice to have that many reasons to throw out the trash every friday. you told me, that night, that you were giving me the promise of your absence and a going away present

> giving me a green glancing blow, sharper and more deadly than the swipe of
> tiresias´s claws

and i was quite surprised because i´d gotten used to never receiving any presents from you, not then, nor at any other time of the year

go on, open it, it´s a bulletin board for your to do lists so that you wouldn´t forget the things that need to be done now that i´m about to leave you. you can even hang a picture of me there…i´ll be keeping an eye on you

and you made me laugh

> cry

just like every morning. so i hung up your photo and my to-do list, but that board became a shadow that i should just as well forget. how can anyone live with the most beloved image of all drilling into her senses with every movement she makes, even in her own home? those are the worst

> and most real

ghosts. that´s why i changed everything around, from the dining room to the kitchen. didn´t you know? there is something deeply moving about kitchens, something far beyond the fruit and knives: it is there you will find the scent of spices you watched grow up from small plants, though hating them, it is there you will find a very large window, illuminating the tile chessboard on the floor, filtering a rainbow parade of light when i wash the dishes,

when i disinfect my tears
by the sink is the calendar and mamá panchita's recipes
    that turn into failures in my hands
the smell of coffee and tiresias's tuna in the morning,
my fingers of syrup and coconut, of annatto or dough; all your photos
stuck to the refrigerator door, as if they were my school homework dis-
played there to celebrate my good grades, though the scores mattered
very little in the end.

i hung the bulletin board in the kitchen on impulse, a whim that grew
from the depths of a premonition, choosing the exactly place where
even tiresias would have to endure your gaze as he passes. you should
look at the board, too, it looks almost new,
    and not, how many years old now?
if lola saw it, she would laugh with her easy, bitter laughter, that she
has surely stolen from somewhere, from someone. your sister is a thief.
only she doesn't realize it. she doesn't notice the heat either and always
dresses in black, even wearing it on her toenails. sometimes it seems
to me that the sun has turned her whole body into one dangerous and
destructive spot, and the only tiny bit of her that hasn't been poisoned
are her mutilated arms, jangling with all the colorful bracelets. i could
erase the darkness, paint over it with a few blue or green brushstrokes,
cover her lips with bright lipstick, and look like a yellow sunflower.
mamá panchita liked yellow
    it brings good luck
        it's liked wrapping yourself up in the virgin of charity's bless-
        ings, copper-colored, with all the sweetness of oshun[1] ...

---

[1] Deity from Santeria who dresses in yellow and is considered a manifestation of the Supreme Being in Yorùbá religions.

but i can't even begin to imagine lola being that illuminated and bright, so full of life. hope must have fled from her body through those cracks in her arms

> by the unhappy death created between her legs.

go on then, you must be tired,

> you must be thinking about the disappointment of carrying yourself on your shoulders. piggybacked

it will do you good to walk, to walk along the avenue filled with flame trees and golden rain, now that the sun is about to disappear. it will be soothing to walk under the cool afternoon clouds without even a single wicked thought forming between your temples. don't worry, i'll always be here

> i always am

i'll take the wooden board, furrowed with cuts and slices, and slide the edge of the knife over each fruit or vegetable, regardless of how large or small they are. i'll dirty my hands with their colors and textures, with the music of the oil boiling in the pan or the slight crackling of the oven turned up to high. i'll make dinner as if getting ready for a party:

> just as i get ready every morning so as not to forget that i can't remember

with care and devotion, with the same tenderness i yank the core out of an apple, its heart, or soften the meat with a mallet. i'll make a dish, the one with the name i can't remember, but that sounds so much like your name, and my fingernails will remain intact, untouched, you'll see, i'll move my hands precisely, flawlessly, and tiresias will come running

> just like you

when the smells from the past, from before, leads him by the scruff of his neck and a swipe from his invisible claws brings you both home again.

Thirteen Ways of Looking at Evening

Jeanne Rana

1. After the heat of the day comes the consolation of evening.
2. Deep purple and lengthening shadows are evening's gown.
3. Evenings can be short or long; most are beautiful.
4. Evening can feel melancholy.
5. What do YOU do when evening comes?
6. Say the word three times—evening, evening, evening. Is it three syllables or two?
7. Evening's cousin "eventually" lives far away.
8. What becomes even in the evening
9. Evening can include a tidying-up, a balancing of the books, a straightening of edges.
10. This housekeeping quality of the word "evening" contradicts the glory of sunset.
11. Many evenings are enchanted.
12. A long evening reminds us of endings, of death.
13. At every moment, evening exists somewhere around the earth, so evening is eternal.

Caravan

Alden Wallace

Though their group is large they make no sound over the biting winds. And none feels like speaking after what had happened earlier. He feels they're being followed, but says nothing. The desert fading into night is like a photo print dissolving back into its negative. Clouds spill over the moon like milk across a nickel on asphalt. Each gust of wind is like a papercut digging deeper into yet an older paper cut. The masochistic flames lick the darkness that will soon consume them. All members of the Caravan sit with a tiny image of the fire in their eyes, staring mutely in return as if in search of their own image hidden somewhere amongst all that heat. Later, winds will take the ash long before it has a chance to cool, and the child will hear his grandmother whisper a single word in her sleep.

What is Fought over in Heaven Falls to Earth

(After a Chinese folktale)

Madronna Holden

The perfect jewel placed
a greedy gleam in the eyes
of the immortals.

They grappled over it—
their fingers greasy
with desire—until
it fell from their hands
and tumbled to earth
to become

the water of our lives.

Then women harbored the pearl
of immortality in their bellies.

Our hearts beat with tides of rubies,
the salt of our tears became crystal;
our happiness, the gems of moisture
in our eyes.

We watered our fields with
the treasure chest of heaven,
drank the silver of the rain,
set our oars into lakes
brimming with diamonds
and rivers running to the
emerald sea.

It should have been enough
to quench our thirst—had we not
also inherited from heaven
that slippery opal of desire.

The Last Party

Katie Lynn Johnston

The flowers in her hair had wilted with the fading of the night, and the scent of tulips from the garden had died along with it as the moon began to rise into the sky. She looked out onto the water and saw their bodies laid bare upon the rocks like melting cream, the folds of their skin molded over muscle and vein and bone, thick as clay, smoothed and softened and wrinkled and plumped like every good thing—and standing there among the reeds, watching them, waiting for a sign, waiting for anything, Hattie smelt the bitter scent of decay and thought perhaps something in her was rotting until she remembered the daisies tangled in her hair and swiped them from her head.

They fluttered to the sands beneath her bare feet, gray and spoilt like dried leaves, and she looked out onto the glittering black sea, the silver moonlight beaming on the women's pale bodies like fruit hidden in the shrouded branches of a tree. The rocks beneath their bare skin were blackened and smoothed, and as the women breathed they seemed to move with them, rising and sinking, like the peaks of their chests, into the sand and back up again.

"Thinking about leaving?" Walt called over the crashing of the waves, his sandaled feet crunching over the reeds, tearing them down like a surge of the sea. His trousers had been rolled up above his knees and his bare legs shone dark in the moonlight.

"No," Hattie called back without looking at him, her eyes upon the silver women, her whole body feeling as if it were sinking into the sands deeper and deeper and deeper past rock and bone and shell through to the groundwater and the dirt, the earth and its hidden caverns and streams, glistening with sharpness.

"Thinking about swimming?" He stood beside her now, flowers woven in his own short hair, and looked down at her as she stared off toward the shore, the light from the house gleaming upon his shoulders. Hattie could hear the roar of the party behind them and felt the air shift as Walt twisted the corner of his collar with his fingertips. His tie was undone, hanging loosely around his neck, his waistcoat unbuttoned, a cigarette, unlit, slack between his lips—he put his hands in his trouser pockets, and Hattie thought he had never looked more ugly.

"No," she said blankly, glancing at him. "No, perhaps tomorrow." She stared back out at the women, draped like linens washed fresh and laid to dry, and she could not help but remember when she was young and afraid, wondering for the kick of anything brighter and more painful than a flame. The air felt as if it was swirling around them now and Hattie could feel the current in the wind, pushing against her ankles, trying to lead her away, closer toward the shore, the women—the lights of the beach house gleaming on the waves. She looked at Walt and she saw him stare out at the sea, his dark eyes shining, the reflection of their bodies lighted within them, and she saw in his face something she had never seen.

"Let us go back," she said quietly, already turning away. Her bare feet stepped carefully around the reeds as Walt, trailing behind her, crushed them into the sand. His eyes glittered with the lights of the house, and she looked up at the terrace, the shadowed bodies of the other houseguests laughing and dancing, spinning through light, as

Doc stood there outside, his hands on the railing, his silhouette black as the sky.

The next morning they went to the water like a flock of sparrows—stripped off their dresses and gowns, leaving them wrapped in the sands of the shore as departed gifts for the wind. The sun was just coming up over the horizon when the first girl crawled upon her rock—and, from her bed, Hattie watched as the yellow light crept upon her dark skin and turned it golden brown like the richest earth in the deepest hole. Soon they all threw themselves upon the rocks and laid out on their smooth blackness, their limbs curled and stretched and spread out in the sun, the blue sky grinning down on them with a strip of hazy cloud. They seemed to be waiting, Hattie thought. For something; anything; a sign; and she wanted to cry out and ask them what it was, what did they see, what did they want, but Walt rolled over. He wrapped his thin arm around her waist in that big white bed, his skin warm and slick against her stomach, and then began to snore. A breeze came in through the open window, white drapes billowing like waves at sea, and the sun crawled over the window ledge, turning the white furniture, the white walls, the white hangings ivory, stains beginning to take form where once they could not be seen.

Outside, the shore was quiet with the current. Still, everyone in Doc's house was sleeping, tossed in their beds, on the floors, wrapped in sturdy rugs or pressed into the creases of wicker lounge chairs. But Hattie couldn't sleep. She hadn't slept since they'd arrived, and she kept having this awful feeling that everything was spreading out around her endlessly like a field sinking further and further into the horizon no matter how close she seemed to come to its edge. She was beginning to worry.

Walt hummed something soft and sweet, and Hattie looked to him. His face was restful and all the tomfoolery of last evening seemed so far from him now—though she could still picture him dancing with his long limbs flying here and there, and sitting then, carelessly, with his legs sprawled, his arms hanging loose over the edge of the sofa as one of the pretty houseguests began picking flowers from the garden and weaving them within his hair. The remnants of last night's bright brocade now hung sadly in his locks, the petals all but emptied, drained, dried.

"Say, what do they do out there, Doc?" Walt asked. He squinted out of the window at the women, far away past the reeds on the shore, the sun blazing in through the glass turning the white walls and furniture and Walt's white clothes bright with the rising light. His fingers were wrapped tightly around his cylindrical glass of ginger ale, but no matter how many times he brought it to his lips, he never took a sip.

"They're preparing for the comet," Doc said, fixing himself a drink at the bar. Ice cubes clinked against the glass. He was grinning at nothing, but his eyes kept darting down to a gray splotch of water on his white suit, distastefully.

"Who are they?" Walt asked, looking back at him.

"I haven't the faintest idea," Doc said, coming up beside him at the window, glass in hand. He took a short swig, his big fingers limply clasping his drink. "There are so many people here...I've never been one for faces. Or mathematics." Doc grinned. He was a giant man and Walt felt horribly small standing beside him. He stood a whole foot taller, and every bit of his muscle and his fat seemed to hang about him, distended as if he had been blown up like the netting on an airship balloon. Walt only nodded in reply, in a way he hoped was congenial, but he watched with interest as Doc's eyes slid over the women on the rocks, a twinkle coming over his large face as his gaze stilled upon the sand.

"Oh, I see," Doc said suddenly and clapped Walt on the shoulder, their drinks jostling. He tapped on the window glass and grinned, but Walt couldn't make out just what he was pointing at—to him, they only looked like so many mounds of skin. "I wouldn't worry, dear Walton, my boy," Doc bellowed. "All women these days have a tendency toward that of the sapphic. What with Maude Adams and all, it's quite in style, truthfully." Doc peeled his hand from Walt's white dress shirt and looked at him with clemency. "I know it must seem—at this moment—quite the trouble, but by tonight—I assure you—you'll have forgotten about it totally." He put his hands in his white trouser pockets and began to trot away, the thick flesh about his neck, which was creased over his suit like the crust of a pie, jiggling as he moved. "I must hurry on now, Walton, my boy. Got to see how Cook's coming along with the desserts for this last party."

Walt nodded and watched him turn the corner and disappear from the large white room, listening abjectly as his footsteps receded down the long hallway, the heat from Doc's hand still on his shoulder.

Out on the rocks, their bodies like candy, Hattie watched the sweat bead on their skin in small glistening pools and felt the noon sun hot on her face. She wandered closer to the shore and sat beneath one of the big black rocks upon the sand and watched the sweat roll down the bends of one woman's arm as it hung over the edge—watched as it danced through the traverses of her skin, the follicles of her hair, the bends of her muscles and her bones, slipping off the tip of her dark fingertip onto the golden sand before her. It left a stain of dark brown, and Hattie thought perhaps she should say something, or else pretend she was sunbathing, too, but she sat still with her legs crossed, watching as each drop of sweat made its dent in the earth and could think of nothing. She had hypnotized herself into nonexistence and, for the first time since she had arrived, she did not feel everything stretching out around her endlessly but the beautiful finality of her own indolence.

By the time she finally found it within herself to go back—standing from the shore, the sand beneath her warm as skin—the clock had already struck half-past two.

She picked her way back up to the house through the reeds, turning every now and again, her hand on her hat, to look back at the women on the rocks as they laid there, still, unmoving. There were forty-two people staying in Doc's house for the end of the world, and Hattie didn't know any of them. They were strewn about the place on white beach chairs, or laid upon the manicured lawn, or else the sofas in the study and the living room like soiled laundry thrown over the back of a chair—the women's hair all disheveled, the men's clothes misplaced, their mouths hanging open with their white teeth shining out like dried pearls in the shell. Hattie tiptoed through their feckless bodies without so much care as not to disturb them as to wake them, but they did not even stir, and by the time she had arrived at the sunroom where Walt had been taking his noon tea, having seen enough of men's undergarments and women's faces smushed into the crooks of each other's necks, their rouged cheeks streaked with stripes of sweat or handprints or tears, Hattie had resigned herself to the expulsion of humanity by whatever means the cosmos saw most fitting.

"Hi, darling," she said.

Walt was squinting out of the window, his fingers pressed against his lips and chin as if he was deep in thought. He glanced over his shoulder at Hattie as she swung down into a wicker chair, but turned back to the glass just as suddenly.

"I must say," Hattie said, taking off her sunhat and examining it as if it was not her own. "We've come for the end of the world, but I've seen nothing so lively yet."

"We have come for today and it has arrived," Walt said absent-mindedly. She glanced at him, but he didn't see.

Hattie put down her hat and placed her thin elbows on the arm-rests of the chair. "What are you looking at?"

"The water." He turned back to her again. "Did you go for a swim?"

"No." Hattie reached for a biscuit on the white tea tray before her, balanced on a pile of old books stacked upon the wicker coffee table. Beneath the teacups she saw the sketch of a woman's face in newsprint, her small eyes glaring out sadly, the earth encapsulating her face as a streak of light-headed toward her thin lips.

"Just to the shore?" he asked.

"Yes," she said, turning her head so she could read the head-line of the paper, her sunhat placed gently upon the round of her knee. She munched on her biscuit, crumbs flitting onto the news-paper and mouthed the words, *Coming Comet Will Collide With Earth May 6 1910*, the sentence feeling funny on her tongue as if it meant nothing.

"I see." Walt turned back toward the window, and again Hattie felt the vast nothingness of life spreading out around her, lifting her from the chair, from her clothes, pulling her into the superfluous sub-sistence of things unseen, into the minuscule realities of dust-mites and peach fuzz and inkblots, the swallowing sensation of actuality sucking her into the floorboards beneath her feet bit by bit, the splinters of the wood pricking every bare part of her body, sticking into her skin as she slipped through each level, passing the figures of the houseguests, all sleeping, as she fell down into the foundations of the house and liquified into the cracks of the stone.

"Oh, Hattie," Walt said softly. She came back to with a rounding shock, grounded into the wicker of the chair. Walt had his head upon her knee and was kissing her fingertips fervently, his eyes lighted with tears, pooling in the small pink corners of their rims. He opened his mouth to speak more, but no sound came out.

"Darling," she said uncertainly. "Dear," she said more assuredly, taking his face in her hands and kissing the top of his head, the scent of dead flowers shrouding his hair in the mug of decay.

The sun had set like the dwindling of a flame and, all day, Hattie saw the women lay still upon the rocks through the window in the sunroom, never moving, hardly shifting, their skin glistening like salt in the sunlight. She saw the houseguests pull themselves up from the ground and the lawn, peel their limbs from the skin of one another, their cheeks and arms decorated with the pinstripes of grass or wicker, their necks puckered with lipstick, chins mucked with drool, as they slumped back to the house and their rooms to ready themselves for dinner and the party. Doc had sent all the men white tuxedos and all the women teal tea-dresses that floated around their skin like clouds, and as Hattie had gotten changed, Walt already gone down to dinner, she'd watched the last discarded gown from the bathers blow away, twisting in the sand as the wind pulled it somewhere else, far away.

"Well, *I* heard," one of the girls sitting across from Hattie on the wicker loveseat in the sunroom was saying, the silver shine of the moon slipping through the windows. Hattie could taste the sugar of dinner on her teeth, and the slick chill of her champagne flute was turning her fingers raw and red like the steak she hadn't eaten. "*They* think they'll soak up the comet's *gasses* with their...*nakedness.*"

The young girl next to her tittered, her shoulders beneath the drapery of her tea-dress bouncing. Behind her head, a buzzing crowd of men in white and women in teal bobbed about the white room with laughter, their heads rising and falling like buoys in the sea, their eyes shining out with the fogged and misty air of stars reflected in water.

"I *don't* believe you," the young one chirped.

"Well, it *is* true," the other said, taking a sip of her champagne, the rim of the glass pressing against her nose.

"*Well*," the young one said with a self-satisfied air, "Have *you* seen that girl who just *sits* there and *watches* them? *I* heard..."

Hattie stood from her seat and moved through the bodies jammed together in the pale sunroom, cigarette smoke fogging the air, the smell of gin and ginger stinging her nose, the lights so yellow and so bright she felt as though she should shade her eyes.

"Now-now, the end of the world can't be as bad as you're think-ing... Why, Doc knows all about these kinds of things," a gray gentle-man was saying to one of the pretty houseguests, his hand resting on her shoulder as she cried into her hanky, her body trembling with each sob. "He does something important in government things, of *course* he knows..."

"Well, I know old Doc works for the ginger ale company," someone else was saying to a crowd of young men, wiping a cloth napkin at his tailcoat. "But I don't see why that means it's got to be the only thing he has in the whole blasted place to drink. If I'd've known the last beverage I'd ever have was..."

"*My* husband was invited by envelope," the pretty lady swung her shoulders back and forth as she spoke. "It had Doc's family crest on it and everything."

"That does sound lovely..." the other said sadly. "Mine only met him in a bar last week and then we came over. Oh...I am glad we did, but..."

Hattie wandered toward the windows, moving slowly through the throng of people as though she hoped they wouldn't notice her. She looked out on the shore, the black ocean rippling calmly with the white light of the moon, full and ripe like a bleached berry hovering just above the horizon. The sky was clear and all the stars were twinkling blindly, the water glittering with their reflections like something Hattie had once seen in a picture shoppe. Out on the rocks, she could still see the women just as they had been when she first saw them that morning. But, now, there was someone else there, too, standing among the reeds, arms hanging loose; head and neck and body seeming all too hollow and sunken-in as if a simple breeze could blow them away. The stranger looked over their shoulder at the house, the terrace, the windows, and Hattie began to feel everything reaching out toward her as if, suddenly, everybody in the room had turned their eyes upon her and were clambering for her through the smokey air, their fingers coming toward her arms and her legs and her chest and her face, not pressing down on her, not holding her, but touching her, softly swallowing her into the smoke and the air like a wave crashing on to the shore.

"They're going out to the water!" someone cried excitedly.

Everyone raced toward the windows, their eyes crazed and watching as the bathers peeled themselves off of the black rocks and strolled toward the shore, languid, heavy in their strides like they had been weighted down and tethered to the earth. Hattie could see only the onlookers' gazes reflected in the glass around her face, jeering, grinning, chattering. With a rush of air, they all stormed out of the room and down the passageways with a resounding clamor, streaming down the stairs, out the doors and open windows like ants, stripping their clothes as they went tumbling toward the shore, their gowns and jackets and underthings sat heavy in the sand like stones. The stranger stood stiffly among the reeds and watched as the people passed by, the men and women crawling toward the water on their hands and knees, through the reeds and the sand, their bare flesh dark in the moonlight, their eyes aglow like animals, like beasts. Hattie watched the stranger gaze upon the crowd as the houseguests swam out to the women and the sea, becoming one mass of indiscernible bodies; and, suddenly, a great streak of light bleared across the sky, leaving a fine fan of silver over the horizon and the moon, the sand and the water and the clothes and the reeds and the grounds lighted with phosphorescence as Hattie's eyes met with the gaze of the stranger standing in the reeds. And then the light vanished. It dwindled away, and Hattie saw her dark face again in the reflection of the window glass, the empty white room behind her littered with champagne flutes and ginger ale bottles and cigarette smoke, her eyes glinting with something she had never seen.

Grave Garden

Elizabeth Wood

I
I imagine your bones,
      white against the earth and
      calm as ashen primrose,
bleached by the fading secrets of morning light.

I imagine you stopping there,
to lie under the kindly plants of your life
      —grasses, maples, Solomon's seal.
      I water a careful patch,
      follow closely as
            small pools gather,
            trickle with disinterest
                  to the far-parched crooks.

I dig down, scan the open earth,
where white larvae pearls clutch jagged roots,
and colonies of reddish ants
harvest with resolve.

Grey-blue earthworm, ringed
with grainy soil
and slime, retreats
        without cause.
A lonely beetle clambers
out from under crusted bark,
        ungainly back exposed and low,
like a hearse: mournful journey home.

II

I imagine your bones, white against the earth,
strong arms that carried us,
bones tough with fear,
bones that rocked us, fed us,
loved,
that strode through life in single file,
whispering a story too quiet to hear.

We take our infant memory bones
from you,
carry their tiny whiteness through this land.

III

How can it hold us, this grief,
amidst all the rebuilding?

Goodbye to What Has Been

Sarah Kain Gutowski

My husband has routine bloodwork drawn
and it's never been more clear that soon
we're going to die, and that maybe that day
is tomorrow, or the next day, or later
this afternoon, in a half hour. First a clot
forms at the injection site, which swells

and blooms a beautiful iris color right
where the elbow cradles the vein.
Then, after the sonogram and the doctor's
well, there's nothing much we can do,
it turns less lovely, a urine stain along
the whiter skin of his inner arm. Within

a few days the results are in: his body
really hates him, and with good reason.
It might rebel at any moment in the most
gauche, uncouth way: stroke, heart attack,
gallstones, failure of liver function. Over
several beers and last hurrah cheeseburgers

we say goodbye to what has been.
At home, my ordinary self is cleaning
the fridge, clearing deli drawers and
freezer shelves of contraband.
My extraordinary self stares wide-eyed
at medical horror stories on the internet.

My inevitable self sits in her chair
by the open window and nods, over
and over again. Her emphatic *I told you
so* mixes with shrill, riotous birdsong.
Our home distends with this noise
and the full, damp, cruel spring air.

The Importance of Staring

Justin Duyao

The mind revels in things like well-laid brick and matching socks—
something about the attention paid to forms, uniforms, structures,
natural or not. For instance, I just met the most beautiful woman,
who, I could tell even from under her mask, had the most incredible
bones. Like an old house you might pass on your bike and note to
yourself, "I've got to come back this way." This isn't love, of course.
More like respectful, limitless fascination. Like Kant says, there is an
eternity in beauty, coiled up in bunches that we believe might uncoil
forever. Of course, they don't. If there's anything we've learned from
the reachings of science, it is that finality is the only thing we can really
grasp anyway—and I mean that literally. That is not to say, however,
that there aren't plenty of things in this world that carry on without
limits: staring, for example. If we let it go on long enough, it toys with
the eternity in things by stretching finality like taffy.

I saw a facade today that had a hard edge where you could see
the architect anticipated there would be another building snugged
up against his, so that one face of his masterpiece was adorned with
Latin etchings and vaulted window sills and the curves of columns
that aren't really columns; whereas the other was smooth, flat, canvas-
like. So the design was bracketed by a beginning and end—but in the
middle, the meat of the sandwich, there was something. Makes me
think about the "Elgin Marbles"—named after the Scottish nobleman

"Lord Elgin," who stripped them from the Athenian Acropolis in 1801 and sold them to the British government in 1816. The British museum, where they remain, maintains that their acquisition was a legal act of preservation. Anyway, makes me think about how the Greeks sculpted these front and back, even though it would be impossible to see their backs from one's vantage on the ground. They had to be perfect—whole. I'm also told Frank Lloyd Wright's *Fallingwater* (1939), a "cabin" he built for friends of his who loved waterfalls, arranges windows where your peripheral vision usually finds walls. Because of this, the mind tricks itself into believing it is out of doors, where the wilderness stretches on and downwards and upwards and sideways forever, as opposed to indoors, where nothing stretches anywhere. You are tricked into feeling the endlessness of the world. Koestenbaum spoke to this in his intimate homage to Forrest Bess (~2012), he said—he pledged, rather—allegiance to "abstract art's Bill of Rights, which contains ... only one provision: the right to look for unstructured amounts of time at migrant and unspecific forms...without demanding that the forms have a single meaning." He calls this "ecstatic surrender" a sort of succumbing to trance. Which, I might add, is exactly what I mean. When we stare, we're allowed endless meanings, endless sensations, endless contradictions piled atop each other like boys in a dog pile.

Socially, of course, staring is strictly taboo. Look too long at a woman's legs, and you have suddenly committed a cardinal sin: the fragmentation of the human body and soul into parts, pieces, objects intended for purposes other than those which God ordained. Something like disintegration in physics, which is a process of decay, or (of a nucleus) to change into one or more different nuclei after being bombarded by high-energy particles, as alpha particles or gamma rays. Rocks become stones by a similar process.

No—women have whole bodies, whole beings which *are* regardless of however their bodies *are*. For instance, look at the woman who is asleep, your lover, she is asleep on the pillow beside yours and her hair is tussled behind her neck, and her breathing is shallow, and she has just kissed you on your forehead because you made a lovely dinner—steak—and stayed up late talking about her coworker—who is a bitch—only you didn't imply this time that you did it because you wanted to have sex, and so she gave it to you willingly, instead of dutifully, and now she is asleep with her hair tussled behind her neck, so it is out of her face and instead into yours, and you loved her once, so you spend time loving her again, for a moment, and then you remember that dick—what was his name—Randy or something, who hit on her once at a bar in Brunswick while you were off getting your lover drinks, only you noticed anyway her flirting right back (in the polite sort of way), her back straight and her eyes soft and red and giggly, like a whisper of affirmation, which is all it takes, and you remember how fucking angry that made you—not the *reality* but the *possibility* of her fucking another guy, even the possibility of her thinking about fucking another guy, the possibility of her entertaining the idea of some fantasy, some other time, while you're out of town on business getting, drinks with coworkers, or at your parents'—whom she never liked—and suddenly, she's definitely fucking Randy when you run to the grocery store and when you step out to grab the mail and when you turn the lights off and saunter upstairs to bed and even, hell, when you blink a little too long. Any moment of inattention is a moment of defeat. So you spend half a decade of your relationship blinking briskly and seldomly because, at any moment, Randy could absolutely enter from stage left. Of course, he never does. She masturbated to him the one time and even by then had forgotten the taste of his name. Only you remembered that. And there it is, his name, and there she is, your lover, breathing shallowly. And there are her legs, a part of her body once again.

Her hair whipped into your face, once, when you were driving down the 101 and you almost drove off the road because it startled you because your mind had drifted off elsewhere. Of course, you didn't drive off the road; instead, you laughed and she laughed and there were the seagulls and the trees bent sideways by years of wind and Big Sur is up ahead—10 miles, max—and so you keep driving, even though you promised she could take over when you got close to Big Sur. You remember gawking at how bare the coastline was between Cambria and Santa Barbara, and you remember her saying the two of you might get a spit of land, one day, in that long empty stretch, and build a house or something so remote they can't send you junk mail, can't knock on your door asking for money for the Girl Scouts, can't smell you smoking weed out the window of your dorm that only opens half a crack to keep sophomores from jumping from the fourth story when their girlfriend leaves them. That was you, once, too brokenhearted and petty and full of all the endlessness of Seasonal Affective Disorder, a cocktail of hormones and self-righteousness and self-doubt. Your lover wasn't around for all that, though. Those were the days when you fell in love with everybody, and everybody fell right back in love with you, where the only thing to do was to flirt (in the impolite sort of way), fuck around about grades, and gripe about town. You watched TV when you were bored, back then. You went to live shows in Memphis on weekdays and skipped class to walk a girl to her job across town. You were also mesmerized by sex, back then, in a way you aren't quite now. Remember? Legs were detached from bodies, back then. As were breasts and smiles and ideas about the future, plans, and such. This was all before you met your now wife, whom you like to call your lover to hold onto all that—anyway, it was she who taught you that sex is meant to be spiritual and practical, all at once, almost like reciting that Lord's prayer or investing in index funds.

All of this comes to you while her chest rises deeply, once, like a sigh, only without anything to say behind it. You love her, now, all of the sudden, again, like you always have—it's funny how we defer to love like it's gravity or something. A universal of human marriage that keeps us grounded, on earth, *in* the earth like roots that grow deeper the more you pull at them. Nothing is more natural about love than the inevitability of detachment. Then again some people pray the Lord's prayer their whole lives, at every mass, at every meal, before bed, before work, before jerking off to the thought of stabbing Randy in the dick. Not the dick, that's impractical. The eyes. Your wife refolded her napkin, once, after finishing a meal and you told her it was ridiculous to assume the restaurant would reuse a napkin after she'd already unfolded it and placed it in her lap, whether she wiped her hands on it or not. She laughed at you, even though you weren't kidding, and said "You don't always have to leave things in such a mess." She was right. You don't. And that's part of why you love her, your lover. She believes there is order in everything, even if you don't. She points out the facades of buildings and has a book on Frank Lloyd Wright. She also walks the dog more times a day than I think even the dog cares to walk, which says an immense amount about her willingness to self-sacrifice. You, on the other hand, would be fine to walk the dog once and spend the rest of the day watching Netflix. You don't watch TV, anymore, by the way. You watch Netflix. Which isn't anything like staring at all.

Ode to Fighting All Weekend

Miles Waggener

Your Sunday apartment,
your chuck eye steaks
winter afternoon of
tell our moment's story,
what is locked away
Your silence turns sated
like an unwelcomed hymn
or being called
a curtain of dust
Through dirty windows
trees look like ashtrays
of ice in bug screens
What newly minted cruelty
to unbolt your door,
Our voices' anger
misunderstandings
reaching for

your balsamic vinegar,
& cigarettes, your embalming
fucking each other, let's not let eternity
shall we? is what you'd say between
& what is released.
but thickens
about a dove or a coin
into a wilderness from behind
motes in blue skillet smoke.
pressed into white vinyl siding,
among the arctic planetary beads
quaking in the wind.
I mutter on my way
I mean.
brings us closer to the small
that make us who we are, our
each other's waists.

Ode to Fighting All Weekend

So tired of ourselves   you make us strangers
but soon we'll eat   food we can't afford
on what used to be   a sewing table & turn
willfully forgetful   of what we were mad about
& why you made us   ever touch each other.
You prod us to keep us   doing anything as hard as we can.

Harmonizing

Sue Fagalde Lick

Downsizing, sorting through old tapes,
she finds "Originals 1983–84," slips it
into her late husband's boombox.

A hum, a fingerpicked guitar, a voice,
high-pitched and clear, singing "Spring Song."
Good God, so chirpy and cheerful.

But there are other tunes begging for love—
"I've Spent a Lifetime Waiting"—and then
"Nobody Makes Me Smile Like You."

Alas, here comes "I Didn't Want to be in Love."
Ah, youth, she fell in love, got dumped,
cried over her guitar. Wrote another song.

She strummed a chord, tasted a phrase in her mouth,
wrote it down and sang it again and again until
the next bit of chorus or verse was revealed.

Completed, she recorded it on a cheap tape
with a tiny plastic microphone plugged
Into a recorder big as a baking dish.

The woman, washing dishes and listening,
harmonizes with her younger self, loving
how the voices blend despite the dust.

As the guitar fingers stumble, she frowns.
Come on, keep going. You can find the note.
All those riffs are easy now. What's hard

is writing a new song to sing.
She dries her hands, picks up her guitar,
strums an A minor chord and sighs.

Learning to Hear Again II

Suzy Harris

The way sound now echoes inside my head—
and all the ticks and taps and dings, unheard before.
Words ring clear and true, but not quite right—
Like everyone is talking from the bottom of a well.

All the ticks and taps and dings, unheard before—
some say like chipmunks, robots, or Mickey Mouse.
For me, it's like everyone is talking from the bottom of a well.
Patience and practice, they say. It will get better.

For some, it's like chipmunks, robots or Mickey Mouse.
Not normal, no, but still a wonder to hear again.
Patience and practice, they say. It will get better—
layers of sound unfolding like an *a cappella* choir.

Not normal, no, but a wonder to hear again.
Words ring clear and true, but not quite right.
Soon, layers of sound will unfold like an *a cappella* choir,
exquisite harmony instead of echoes inside my head.

Something Like That

William Cass

After I got my administrative credential, I was hired to be one of the assistant principals at the high school where I'd been a PE teacher and girls' basketball coach. My new position involved a variety of site and district-level duties, but one I hadn't expected to face so early on occurred in mid-November when my supervisor, our school principal, told me I needed to take her place on an expulsion hearing panel. She barged into my office shortly before dismissal and apologized for the short notice, but said she'd just gotten a call that her young son had broken his arm in a playground accident. She'd cleared my taking her place at the hearing with the head of the panel, a cold, gruff man named Carl Peterson who was the Assistant Superintendent of Student Services. She told me it would start in a half-hour, then hurried out of my office as quickly as she'd entered it.

I sat blinking for several moments afterward as I stared at where she'd been, a slow wave of dread crawling up through me. I knew about that expulsion case because one of our school's other assistant principals had initially handled the incident. It involved a student on our boys' basketball team and its coach with whom I'd worked for many years. Our practice courts and locker rooms had been right next to one another's. I'd long cringed at the way he berated his players, the shouts, the cursing; I'd even heard he'd sometimes put his hands on them. The boy being brought up for expulsion, a senior and star player named Brad Holland, had slugged him during practice the week before and broken his nose. The other assistant principal said Brad had told him he'd just lost it after all the coach's abuse. "That may have been the case, but the kid crossed a line," my colleague said and then chuckled. "Suppose you could say this expulsion is a slam dunk."

I got to the conference room adjoining the district office boardroom where the hearing was to be held a little more than twenty minutes later. Carl and the other two admins on the panel, the Human Resources Director and a principal at a neighboring high school, were already seated around its rectangular table. Both men were longtime and highly-regarded administrators who'd been part of the interview team that had selected me for my new position. I'd just turned thirty-two, and they each had three decades on me. We mumbled greetings, then Carl pointed to an empty chair. He told me to close the door first, which I did, before slumping obediently into the vacant seat. Carl immediately began reviewing the case's essential ingredients with us; they were basically the same as what my colleague had told me. He then gave us copies of the district's Discipline Action Guide, which all students and parents had to sign during registration, with an asterisk next to the related guidance that read: "Although administrators have some discretion, expulsion will generally be recommended for these offenses:" A bulleted list followed, the last of which was "assault or battery upon any school employee" (Education Code Section 48915 (a)).

After we'd read it and looked back up, Carl said, "Trusting you'll agree this particular case is pretty straightforward. No real gray area." From the corner of my eye, I saw the other two admins nod. "So, this is how it will go," Carl continued. "We'll introduce ourselves, and I'll explain who you are on the panel and that your decision on the case must be unanimous and is final, no appeals permitted." He lifted the Discipline Action Guide. "Everyone will have a copy of this, which I'll read aloud, and then I'll very briefly present the district's case for expulsion. Next, the student or his parent, if he has one with him, can say whatever they like in defense. After that, we leave the room and wait in the hallway so the three of you can confer. That shouldn't take long given the circumstances here. When you're done, you come get us, we sit back down, and one of you states your collective decision. Then we all go on our merry ways." He cocked his head. "Any questions?"

The principal said, "None."

The HR Director stood up. "Let's get this over with."

The boardroom was arranged with two long tables facing each other separated by a half-dozen feet. Three chairs were behind one, and four were behind the other nearest to the doors. At the far end of that table, Brad and a squat, stocky woman I assumed to be his mother were seated with their backs to us. They turned and watched us as we entered. Brad was dressed in dark pants with a dark shirt and tie, his long, lean frame draped over the chair and his eyes following us as the other two admins and I made our way to the seats at the empty table; I took the one in the middle. Carl settled himself into the chair at the end of their table, cleared his throat, and introductions were made; as suspected, the woman with Brad said she was Mrs. Holland, his mother. Then Carl started the proceedings. When he slid Discipline Action Guides to Brad and his mother, she frowned deeply. As Carl read, I watched her reach under the table and pat Brad's knee. He folded his arms and stared at the carpet. I didn't know him well, but he'd been in an off-season weightlifting class I'd taught a couple of years earlier and hadn't seemed like a bad kid. Quiet, sort of reserved, a hard worker; he'd been recruited at a small college nearby where I'd played myself. A kid with a bright future and loads of potential. When Carl got to the part about assault and battery, Brad shook his head slowly back and forth.

Next, Carl made his case for expulsion. True to his word, he was short and to-the-point. I took notes as he spoke; the other two admins sat motionless next to me. When he'd finished, he asked if Brad or his mother had anything to say.

"I do," Mrs. Holland said and stood up. "You can't expel my son. What he did wasn't right, but he was forced into it. That coach berated him and those other players like you wouldn't believe...just pushed and pushed and pushed. Brad had more than three years of it, the resentment of it, the unfairness building and building. So, when that coach called him vulgar names at that practice, his spittle spraying in Brad's face, my son, well, just snapped." She paused, looked down at Brad with his folded arms and dour expression, then at each of us. "So, please, extend his suspension, add on community service, anything, but don't kick him out of school. He graduates in six months and has a college basketball scholarship waiting for him that will go up in smoke if he's expelled. You can't rob him of that for a single provoked mistake."

Mrs. Holland sat back down. Carl let a few seconds pass before he said, "I'll just remind the panel again that this student punched his coach, a school employee, in the face and broke his nose."

"That son-of-a-bitch got what he deserved," Brad hissed. He'd raised his head and had sat up straight, his eyes narrowed. "You don't know the half of it. Brought a skirt to practice for whoever lost a rebounding drill to wear. Shoved our point guard into a locker after we lost a game because he turned the ball over too much. Told me during that practice I was the first faggot he'd ever made a captain."

"That's hearsay," Carl said. "And not pertinent to the incident being considered." He waved his Discipline Action Guide. "Punched his coach. Broke his nose."

"I think we've heard enough," the HR Director said.

The principal nodded. "I agree."

"Fine," Carl said. "The three of us will wait in the hallway while you confer."

When he stood up, Brad and his mother followed suit. Before turning to leave, Brad leveled each of us with a troubled glare. Before his gaze reached me, I had trained my eyes on the additional notes I was pretending to scribble. I kept scribbling until I heard the board-room doors click shut behind them.

After they left, several moments of silence went by before the HR Director said, "So, I'm ready to vote. Guilty as charged."

The principal nodded again. "That coach sounds like a piece of work, but I vote the same. A student simply can't punch a school employee."

They both turned and looked at me until the HR Director finally said, "Well?"

"I don't know." I'd hoped to sound stronger, but I could barely get the words out. Nausea rose from my belly. I knew that by morning our decision and my complicity in it would be common knowledge across the district. And my future administrative career would certainly be affected by my hand in this decision, one way or another. I had many years of work ahead of me; my wife and I had just stretched our budget to buy our first home on the heels of my higher salary.

"Listen, son," the HR Director said to me, "there's strong precedent to consider here. Think about what this decision says to the next student who gets pissed off at a teacher or another staff member."

"He's right," the principal said. "No question about it."

They each looked at me with set jaws. My temples pounded. The silence in the room seemed deafening.

Finally, I nodded once and muttered, "Okay, sure."

The HR Director clapped me on the back. "Good," he said. "I'll go get them."

I didn't look up when they were all seated at their table again and the HR Director delivered our decision, but I heard Brad grunt and his mother begin to cry. I continued to stare down at my notes while everyone gathered their things and left the room. Brad and his mother were the last to leave. Afterward, I sat alone in the dwindling, late afternoon vaguely aware of traffic passing in the street outside.

When my wife got home from work an hour or so later, she found me sitting in the gathering darkness at the dining room table, an empty beer bottle in front of me and another nearly empty one in my hand. The table wasn't set and no meal had been started; whoever got home first always did those things.

She stopped a few feet away and said, "Hi there."

"Hey."

She came over next to me, lifted the empty beer bottle, and said, "Got a little head of steam going. Tough day?"

I shrugged.

"What happened?"

"Hard to explain."

"Involve a kid?"

I nodded. "A boy." I managed to hold her gaze. "I fucked up with him. Made a lousy decision."

She nodded slowly herself. The look she gave me reminded me of the one she'd fixed me with during her speech at our wedding rehearsal dinner when she said what she admired most about me was my integrity. The knot in my stomach seized. She squeezed my shoulder and said, "You'll make it right."

I lowered my eyes. "Don't see how."

"You'll think of something."

Neither of us said anything then while a siren started from the fire station down the street. She waited until the sound of it had died away to say, "Well, how about if I heat up some leftovers for dinner. That sound okay?"

"Sure."

I still hadn't looked back up at her. She squeezed my shoulder again and went into the kitchen.

I tried to chase away thoughts of the expulsion hearing but didn't sleep much that night. Things weren't much better the next morning when I heard the boys' basketball coach crowing to other teachers about the expulsion decision in the staff lounge. Worse yet, later that afternoon, I passed the gym on my way to the parking lot and heard him hollering at his players in practice.

I'd left work as early as possible and stopped at a bar near our house on my way home, something I never did unless I was joining other staff members for an occasional TGIF. The place was narrow, low-lit, and mostly empty, just as I was feeling. I took a stool on the far end and nursed a vodka cranberry while I let my thoughts tumble over themselves. I couldn't shake the sound of Mrs. Holland's first choked sob after the HR Director had delivered our decision or the look in Brad's eyes as he'd made his tortured outburst beforehand. I thought about when I'd been a small boy and had let a classmate be punished for stealing a knit cap from the coatrack when I knew another student, the class bully, had done it. I'd kept silent then, too; I hadn't had the courage to speak up. I found myself slumping forward, my eyes shut tight.

Over the next few weeks, I regularly checked the log our secretary kept whenever records were requested for a student transferring to a different high school, but Brad's name never appeared on it. I also called a few alternative high schools in the area where he could have completed his GED, but he hadn't enrolled in any of them either. Thanksgiving and Christmas breaks provided distractions that kept me from thinking as much about him and the expulsion, as did the gradual accumulation of time, but those thoughts were never far away, like muted clouds always lurking. I pushed harder and longer on my morning runs, but that didn't help. Sometimes, my wife found me lying awake next to her in bed late at night and asked if I was still thinking about that kid; when I just rolled over and didn't answer, she'd wrap her arm around me and snuggle close.

I did my best not to let any lingering preoccupations about Brad affect my work at school. I was in charge of all our standardized testing, which ratcheted up in February, so the challenge of coordinating all of that, as well the data analysis sessions that followed each test, kept my mind preoccupied most of the time until the end of the school year. Ours was the only site in the district with no testing compliance violations. I'd always been good at organizing things of that sort and analyzing data, areas key to what made me successful as a basketball coach. I guess senior administration took notice, too, because they appointed me as the temporary replacement for the district's Assessment

Coordinator when she left on maternity leave in June. That meant working through the summer, which I was happy to do to stay busy, as well as extra pay, which pleased my wife.

When the new school year began, the Assessment Coordinator decided to resign in order to stay home with her new baby, and her position became permanently mine. A jump from assistant principal directly to the district office was almost unheard of, so a lot of kudos came my way. I admit that I did bask a bit in the comforting waters of professional validation. But I shuddered when Carl Peterson stopped in to congratulate me on the permanent appointment saying he knew from the start that I was destined for big things. Like I also did when, driving home from work, I sometimes saw a bicycle with a tall seat and handlebars like the one Brad used to ride leaning up against an abandoned building in a shady part of town. Or, when a small boy from up the street walked by the front of our house wearing a knit cap almost identical to the one that had been stolen from that classroom of my youth.

Just before Thanksgiving break, not quite a year to the day of the expulsion hearing, when I was returning a shopping cart to its rack in a grocery store parking lot, I felt a chill as a woman's voice behind me said, "I'll take that if you're done with it."

I turned slowly, and Mrs. Holland's eyes rose to meet my own. They narrowed like her son's had at the hearing, and I watched her stiffen. She said, "You."

I swallowed and heard myself say, "How's Brad?"

"Awful, after what you people did to him." She was breathing quickly through her nose, her chest rising and falling. "Gone to hell, if you want to know the truth."

"I hoped he'd finish school somewhere else. Maybe play ball at a JC."

"Never went to class again, never picked up another basketball. Was just lost, got in with a bad crowd, started using." Her eyes had widened and her bottom lip began trembling. "He's at Caron now, thanks to you."

I was familiar with the name of the rehab center; I'd known a few other students who'd ended up there over the years. An image flitted across my mind of Brad hitting the free throw that iced the section championship during his junior year, followed by the swarm of teammates mobbing him afterward as time expired and the din of cheers from the stands. The stiffness evaporated from Mrs. Holland, and her shoulders sagged. A kind of numbness filled me.

"I'm sorry," I said. "For whatever it's worth, I've felt awful ever since that hearing. I made a terrible mistake. I shouldn't have voted for expulsion. But I didn't speak up, didn't have the guts. I'm so sorry. So very, very sorry."

Along with anger, something new filled Mrs. Holland's eyes, some combination of weariness, resignation, hopelessness. "Try telling that to Brad," she said. It came out as almost a whisper. Then she walked past me towards the store, leaving the cart I still gripped behind her.

It took me a week to gather the nerve to go to the rehab center. My wife and I were on our way to meet some friends near it for dinner, and I told her I just had to run inside for a minute. I ignored her frown as I parked at the curb in front of the building and left the car.

I wasn't even sure Brad would still be there, but when I asked the receptionist, she said she'd let him know he had a visitor. She pointed to a little room to her right. A small table filled most of it. I sat in the chair facing the door and rubbed my forehead. Music played faintly somewhere through the walls.

A few minutes later, Brad appeared in the open doorway and stopped. We looked at each other for a long moment, his face expressionless. Finally, he said, "What do you want?"

I pulled back the chair next to me, but he shook his head. I blew out a breath and said, "I came to apologize. I shouldn't have voted to have you expelled. I've felt horrible about it every day since."

Nothing in his face changed. He was wearing jeans, a baggy blue T-shirt, and the same high-top sneakers that had been issued to all the school's basketball players. He looked like he'd lost weight. His eyes stayed on mine, but he remained silent.

I asked, "How're you doing? Here, I mean."

He scowled. I nodded slowly, then took out some folded papers from my jacket pocket and pushed them across the table in his direction.

He looked from the papers to me and said, "What are those?"

"The district next to ours has started a new online continuation program. I went over your records with the director, and he thinks you can get enough credits to graduate in a few months if you work at it hard enough. I registered you. Didn't need your mother's signature because you're eighteen now. I'm guessing you have some free time here and access to a computer, so you could start right away." I pointed to the papers. "The username and password are there on top."

He looked down at the papers again and shook his head.

"And I talked to the coach at the college that offered you a scholarship. He's actually an old friend of mine; we were teammates there. I explained things to him, including the expulsion hearing, how it should have gone down. He says there'd be a spot for you on the team in the fall if you get your diploma, finish rehab, stay clean."

Brad stood very still in the doorway staring at me. "Why are you doing this?"

"Because I screwed up and you got screwed up because of it. Because that old coach of yours is an asshole and shouldn't be working with kids. Because I owe you. Because I want to see you do well."

"Big guilt trip, huh?"

I hesitated, then said, "Something like that, I guess."

He took a turn at nodding slowly, then reached over and picked up the registration papers. I watched him roll them into a tube, and then he was gone. Dust floated in the wan shaft of sunlight where he'd been standing. The music had stopped. I looked out the room's window where heavy-bellied clouds gathered with the setting sun over the treetops. It looked like it might rain. I hoped it would and that would help wash things away.

When I got back in the car and had started the engine, I could feel my wife's eyes steady on me.

She said, "Take care of everything?"

I looked over at her and shrugged.

She gestured with her chin toward the rehab center. "That the boy you've been worried about?"

My nod was short.

"Things better?"

I shrugged again. "Hope so."

She put her hand on top of mine. Her lips pursed before she said, "Regret's a hard pill." She paused. "I'm sure you did your best..."

Her voice trailed off. She shrugged herself. I tried to smile, but it felt feeble. So, instead, I brought the back of her hand to my lips and kissed it.

September Coastal Midnight

—Near Dam Neck, Virginia. If the map didn't lie.

Jeffrey Alfier

Thunder shook me from sleep. I blinked hard
to know this dark will not drown me

in a lack of light, that the hazy bottle
of Riesling holds its gentle emptiness

under hardwood blinds that sag
like the victim of a stroke, the sea

unwearied in tidelines beyond my sight,
the late summer dawn to arrive once more,

blossoming over the surf, that a kind woman
still slumbers warmly beside me

knowing the winsome years are behind me,
the rain still falling over the vacant streets.

Tenth Month

Andrea Campbell

The first happiness was a short six-hour labor and the sight of all 10 pounds 2 ounces of you.

The second happiness—deciding on the spot that I would keep you with me always never minding what the outside world would say.

The third the length of time that you and Jane were close and she protected you. It lasted really all the years until your size was more than hers.

The fourth happiness was how you found a way to grab your strength when you were dropped into a world of different color and you learned that all the fields of sport were yours for taking.

And the fifth became your closest friends who fell asleep on porches waiting for you, swam in summer rivers with you, friends you had and lost and never found again.

Sixth was when your dad began to be your dad and when we moved to Portland where you didn't feel so lonely for his part of all your ancestors and history.

And now I have to rest a bit because the sadness has to have its share before I circle back and think of happiness again.

Learning Patience

Sarah Kain Gutowski

My inevitable self isn't very precious or careful
about her body and where she places it,
which means that sometimes we find her frozen
in various parts of the house, waiting for someone
to come to her rescue. Neither my ordinary self
nor my extraordinary self can respect that,

but then, they've never been good at asking
for help. My inevitable self has learned patience,
and will wait out the spasm in her lower back
or hang, importuned and limp as an afghan,
over the couch arm, until a passing child
or adult passes by. *Give us a push*, she'll say,

or extend an arm for us to take and pull.
Once, we find her trapped beside the oil burner
in the basement; for hours we've mistaken
the tapping of her cane for the pinging of water
moving through pipes. *How'd you end up here*,
my ordinary self says, shaking her head

with closed eyes to show her deep disapproval
and disdain, while my extraordinary self
navigates between the copper extensions
to the place where she'll have leverage.
My inevitable self laughs under her breath,
thwacks her cane against the water heater,

and ends my ordinary self's pantomime.
It doesn't matter how I happened here,
or how you found me, numbnuts.
She braces her spine and grunts against
my extraordinary self's assistive push.
Instead, ask: what will I do, what will we do,

now that we've found ourselves
in this position? She extends her arms toward
my ordinary self and beckons. My ordinary self
accepts those outstretched hands and pulls,
and, smocked in cobwebs and cricket legs,
my inevitable self rises. *See*, she says. *It's easy.*

Round Trip

Phil Harvey

Brian's fifty-fifth birthday party had been, well, pretty good. At Jillian's suggestion, Dain Thorson's wife had made a cake, two cakes really, each shaped like a five, recognizable but not exactly graceful. The cake part, inside, had been delicious. They had all endured Jillian's brother's loud and repeated clichés about the "double nickel" birthday and the importance of observing speed limits. Now the guests were gone. The gas fire was burning under the fake logs in the fireplace, a feature of the house that Brian didn't like, but Jillian would not have all the dust and ashes blowing around from real wood fires.

When the last guest was out the door, Jillian turned, facing Brian in the living room, her hands pressed against her hips in a posture of someone having successfully completed a task.

"Well," she said. "That turned out pretty well, didn't it?"

"It sure did," Brian said. "It sure did."

"Well," Jillian said again. "Special occasion. Major birthday." She paused, looked around, and glanced at her husband, a warm expression. "Would you like me to rub your back?"

Brian smiled. "Yes. Good. That would be nice." They sidled over in front of the fire with the metal logs. With a practiced move, Jillian pulled three of the big square pillows from the couch and pushed the coffee table to the side, making a bed for Brian in front of the blue and yellow flames. He eased himself down on the pillows with a quiet sigh, stretched his arms out above his head, and waited.

"There, baby, there," she whispered, softly repeating the phrase in time to the gentle pushing and probing of her fingers. She sat with her legs straddling him, pressing close.

"I don't think they like me very much at work," Brian said, his voice muffled in the pillow.

"Sure they do, baby. Sure they do. Dain likes you."

"He's my friend," Brian said. "But he's the only one." He paused as her fingers pressed against him. "Yesterday I heard Gina laughing in the hallway," he said. "I looked out, uh, and she said four of them were going to lunch at the Brown Torch and…" He waited to match his breathing with the rhythm of his wife's hands. "And did I want to join them? But she didn't mean it. She just asked because…I was there. Most of them are, uh, younger than me."

"Shh," Jillian whispered. "They respect you." She pushed close against him. "Let me tell you a little story." She shifted now, hiking up her skirt on either side with her knees pressing against his rib cage, left and right. She began a new, more insistent rhythm, pushing forward, her hands against his back as she rocked back and forth. "There once was a very intelligent man who was good with numbers," she said. "He was the most respected man at his office." Brian sighed. "When there was an especially difficult accounting problem, they came to this man because he was the best…"

She shifted again, pressing herself down against him. He could feel the soft area between her legs, warm, dark, pressing against his back. "The man could always solve their problem…"

"Yes," Brian said. "He could…solve the problem." He sighed again. Now, tentatively at first, then with increasing firmness, he could feel the heel of her left hand pressing into the center of the small part of his back. Her other hand was between her legs, stroking. They rocked gently against each other, and after a few moments, Jillian let out a long breath and stopped moving. Then they resumed the rhythm until a high-pitched cry came from the place where Brian's face was buried in one of the pillows.

Now Jillian raked her fingertips smoothly over his back, the serious massaging finished. "You should probably replace this shirt," she said. "The neck is starting to fray."

"What size shirt do I wear?" he said.

"Fifteen and a half, thirty-three."

"What does that stand for?"

"Neck circumference and sleeve length," Jillian said.

"Oh," he said.

"Would you like to learn things like that? Your jackets are forty-two regular. Your shoe is an eight and a half D. Your waist is thirty-eight."

"How do you know all that stuff?"

"I take care of you. I've always taken care of you, haven't I?"

"Yes," Brian said. "You've always taken care of me."

The next morning at breakfast, Brian poured skim milk over his bran flakes and then, after a hesitation, he added a small dollop of whole cream from the coffee creamer. Jillian looked at him quizzically but said nothing. She watched as her husband ate.

"I really think you should start buying your own clothes, Brian," she said finally.

"You think so?"

"Don't you? Don't you think so?"

"Oh, I suppose so," Brian said. "I suppose I should."

"Why don't you start by buying your shirts? You need two new ones. They have them at J. Press. The kind you like."

"What if they ask me questions?"

"What could they ask?" She was quiet for a moment. "If they ask if you want the regular cut or the trim cut, you want the regular cut. Never get 'trim' or 'slim' in anything. Trim is for those youngsters with twenty-six-inch waists."

"Anything else?"

"I don't think so," she said. "I think that covers it."

The next day Brian returned from work with a shopping bag that said "J. Press" on the side, blue with gold lettering. "I did it," he said. "I got both shirts. I got an extra one too."

"Let's see," Jillian said. They went into the living room, where late afternoon sunlight pooled on the couch in front of the fireplace. Brian pulled out the three shirts, still in their paper-band wrapping, and held them up one at a time. Jillian was silent, scowling.

"What's the matter?" Brian said.

"You don't wear stripes," she said.

"Just one with stripes. I thought it would be interesting."

"You always wear solid colors. Blue or white. You don't wear stripes."

"I thought it would be fun, just this once."

"You don't wear stripes."

Brian paused for a moment. Then he said, "I'll take it back. I only need two shirts anyway. Two is plenty. One white one and one blue one. Makes a total of eight for the office. I'll take the striped one back in the morning."

Two weeks later, Brian invited his friend Dain to lunch. As they finished their coffee, Brian reached for his wallet. "Omigod," he said. "I left my credit card at the office." He looked again to be sure.

"I'll use mine," Dain said. "You can give me a check."

"A check?"

"Sure. I'll pay the bill, and you give me a check. Easy."

"I don't know," Brian said. "I have a check, but..."

"Yes?"

"I never write checks on our joint account. Jillian wouldn't be able to balance it in her register. She keeps track. She pays the bills. She..."

"No big deal," Dain said. "Pay me when you have the cash."

"No," Brian said. "This meal's on me. My treat. That's the deal." He paused briefly. "I'll give you the check. I can tell her about it tonight." He pulled a folded check from his wallet. It was a little brown, the edges curled, but it was intact. Brian had already entered the word "emergency" on the memo line.

He gave Dain the check: $56.50, including tip. Brian noted the amount and check number in the back of his planner.

"I wrote check number 1106 for $56.50 to Dain for lunch today," he said to Jillian that night. "Is that okay? I left my credit card at the office by mistake, and I promised Dain I'd buy him lunch, to celebrate the close of the Millman Charity audit."

Jillian looked at him briefly, then said, "Sure. Let me get the checkbook. I'll make a note." When she returned, he repeated the information. She said, "You've never written a check on this account before."

"I know. I considered this an emergency. It was my invitation to lunch."

"Why don't you open an account of your own?"

"My own account?"

"Sure. Part of the independence thing, like buying your shirts."

"That didn't turn out so well."

"Sure it did," she said. "You got the shirts, they fit fine."

"That's true," he said. He looked out the window. "What's my size again?"

"Fifteen and a half, thirty-three."

"My own checking account," he said in a quiet voice. "That's an interesting idea."

"You may even be able to get a toaster or something," Jillian said. "For opening a new account."

"My own checking account..." He looked up. "How will I fund it? I give you my paycheck for the joint account. There isn't a lot of surplus."

"Sure there is," she said. "I put a thousand dollars in our IRA every quarter. I could make it a little less."

"Oh, I don't know," he said. "I wouldn't want to cut back on that."

"We won't be spending any more money, Brian. That won't change. But you'll have some money you control on your own instead of paying everything through me."

"How much could we put in?"

"Say fifteen percent of your take-home pay, after tax. That should be safe enough."

"Fifteen percent...and anything else still goes to the joint account?"

"Of course," she said.

"Fifteen percent." He paused. "Well, let's try it. I'll give you my check on payday. I'll calculate the fifteen percent, and you can give me a check for that amount for my personal account."

"Sure."

"Well, okay," he said. "We'll try it."

The following April 23rd, Brian's firm awarded a series of unexpected bonuses to mark the end of the tax season. Brian received a check for $2,800. He examined the check, and left work on the dot of five, unusually early for him. He went straight to the Central Union Bank on the corner, conveniently close to the lot where he parked his car, and went to one of the little island tables in the middle of the open floor. He carefully tore a deposit slip from the back of his new checkbook, filled it out, endorsed the bonus check, and handed it in at a teller window. He collected his receipt and went back to the table. He checked again to be sure that he had made the appropriate entry in his check register with the correct date. Then he folded the receipt in half and tucked it inside the checkbook cover flap.

On the way home that evening, he debated with himself. The prospect of a secret amount in his own account was powerful. Jillian had urged him to get the new account to be more independent. With the bonus, his independence would go way up, especially, he thought, if he kept this information to himself.

Still, he should tell her. It might make it possible to increase their IRA contribution.

He decided to wait. He'd wait and see. If it seemed appropriate, he'd tell her over the weekend.

A few weeks later, on a warm, sunny morning, Brian noticed something new in the Brooks Brothers' display window on the way to his office. It was a brightly colored summer sport jacket, vaguely plaid with bright pastels in carefully matched patch-like combinations, visually eye-catching, almost the antithesis of Brooks' traditional conservative suiting. The jacket wasn't gaudy, but it would certainly stand out in a crowd. All those colors!

The Brooks Brothers store was just halfway between the lot where Brian parked his car each morning and his office, two doors down from the Union Bank. He passed the display window every workday. The second time he passed the new display, he took a long look at the bright madras jacket and smiled to himself. Not for him! The next day he stopped again and shook his head at the "coat of many colors," pleased that he so easily recalled the Bible story about Joseph. That coat got Joseph into trouble, Brian remembered.

The following day he stopped again to look, and on the next day, he went inside to try the jacket on. The following Monday, on his way home from work, he bought the jacket in a size forty-two regular, which he had written down in his planner. It fit him perfectly.

Jillian burst out laughing. "You can't be serious," she said.

"I like this jacket," he said. "Different. Something special."

"It sure is," Jillian said. "But you can't wear it out in public."

"Why not?"

"It doesn't suit you. It's not in keeping with your character. It's not what you do." She stared at him, her expression serious now.

"I like it," he said.

"What did it cost?"

"Five hundred eighty-seven fifty, including tax."

"You'll have to take it back." She paused briefly. "Where did you get that much money?"

"I...I got a bonus."

"A bonus? How much? When?"

"Twenty-eight hundred. April 23rd."

"And you didn't tell me?"

"I forgot." Jillian stared. Brian looked away.

"This has gone too far, Brian," she said. "You'll take the jacket back. We'll close the new account. I can't keep track this way."

"No," he said.

"You listen to me…"

"No!" he said again. He looked at her. "You said I should be more independent. It was you who said I should buy my own clothes, and the bank account—"

"I didn't say you should lie to me."

"I didn't lie. I forgot to mention it."

"You lied to me. You got a bonus and covered it up. You bought that ridiculous coat—"

"It's not ridic—"

"That ridiculous coat, and ruined the family accounts; our finances are in shambles. I won't have it."

"No!" Brian's voice was sharp, determined. "I won't take this back." He held the jacket in front of his chest, like a shield.

"You won't wear it," she said, and she walked into the kitchen, returning with the heavy kitchen scissors.

"No," he said.

She cut the coat upward from the bottom, then grasped the cut edges and ripped the jacket apart, placing the scissors carefully on the table. Brian held the jacket out away from him, stared at the long, jagged tear that split the left side in half right up to the lapel pocket. "No," he said, and a high-pitched wheezing sound came from his throat. He stood a full minute, trembling, holding the coat against his chest. Then, very slowly, he put the jacket down on the dining table and stared at it. "I don't think they like me at work," he said. "They don't like me."

"Sure they do, baby," she said. "Sure they do." She looked at him, friendly now. "Come here, baby," she said gently. "Let me tell you a little story." She moved to the overstuffed chair in the corner of their living room, a quiet, sheltered spot.

Brian came to her and sat on the carpet at her feet. "Come here," she repeated, patting the side of her leg to indicate where he might rest his head. Brian settled on the floor and leaned his head back against her knee, emitting a sigh. Slowly and carefully, she stroked his forehead and his temples. "There once was a very smart man who was good with numbers," she said. "He worked long and hard, sometimes putting in two or three extra hours in a day, sometimes ten or twenty extra hours in a week, to make sure that they were absolutely accurate, in every respect."

"That's true, that's true. The numbers must be correct in every respect."

"This man worked so hard and so conscientiously that they sometimes made fun of him, calling him a 'workaholic.' But when they needed something done, when there was an important deadline, who did they come to?"

"They came to him. They came to the conscientious man. They came to the man they made fun of."

Her voice was low and soothing, and as the story went on, she let her legs move apart, a few inches at a time.

"So this man did his duty," she said. "He made his department better and more productive. He was a good man. And when he was gone, they all began to say, 'Whatever happened to so-and-so? I'll bet so-and-so could solve this problem.'"

She pulled his head gently toward her until his mouth touched the inside of her thigh. She whispered now. "The bank account must be closed." Brian pushed his tongue against the soft skin on the inside of her thigh.

"At the office," Brian said. "About so-and-so." He pressed his elbow gently against the hardness at the front of his pants.

"Yes," she said. "They said, 'If so-and-so were here, I'll bet we wouldn't be in this mess. If only so-and-so were back, I'll bet things would be a whole lot better. Why didn't we appreciate so-and-so when he was here?'"

Jillian eased her husband's head to the side, leaned forward, and stood up, bending slightly. Brian watched, his head resting against the chair, as she pulled up her skirt, stripped off her underpants, and sat back down, her legs swinging apart. She touched the back of his head and looked at him. "The bank account must be closed," she said. Brian pushed his lips gently against her soft, yielding skin. He made a gentle humming sound and moved higher, between her legs. She pushed her fingers carefully into his hair, pulled his head back until she could look into his eyes. Softly she said, "The bank account must be closed."

"Yes," he said. "I'll go there tomorrow, first thing. I'll close it."

"At the office," she said. "They were saying that so-and-so had held things together. He kept the department on a steady keel. He was the best senior accountant they ever had."

Brian's head moved, just slightly. "Yes," he said, his voice muffled. "The very best they ever had."

Two Portraits of Widowhood

Marisa P. Clark

*In his loneliness, he cut grass
and drank beer.* This is my mother
speaking. *Randy came over
to check on him and they drank
beer.* My mother reclines
in Dad's leather chair, phone
propped on her chest, a plastic cup
of water near. *He was drinking
a lot of beer.* When my grandmother
had been dead three months
or four, they took her clothes
to the firepit and burned them
one by one—cotton housedresses,
nightgowns, undergarments. *Mama
wouldn't have wanted anyone else
to have her things, I don't think.*

The buttons must have melted.
Did the zippers melt too, or did
their silver teeth survive the fire?

In assisted living, my grandfather
was popular. Dapper, blue-eyed,
walked without a cane. Had a car,
had his mind, had no need
for an oxygen tank to help him
breathe. Called the dining room
the mess hall, called his closet
the locker. Otherwise, he never
talked about the Navy or the war.
One night after a party,
he had to be wheeled to bed—
two beers had him flying
high. One day he visited Delores
in her room but left because
she wore a bra, no blouse.
One day my mother found
lipstick on his collar and fussed
him into shame. He played
poker for pennies. Drove friends
to the casino, drove alone to spend
time with my grandmother's tombstone.
One evening, the sprinklers came on
and he got soaked trying to run.
These memories are mine.

On the phone, my mother's still
riffing about Randy and the sale
of the house and land. This is how
she followed up another promise

to speak no more of her own death
and what I'm to do with her
possessions and cremains. *I'm ready,*
she said at the start. *When I go,*
you're to remember I was ready.

Lost Birds

Cheryl Waitkevich

There are notices for a missing cockatiel on the telephone
poles.

usually it's a cat, lounging
in their owners arms eyes
betraying

the pleasure of being held,
Or swishing tail up
waiting

for more food—you know—
pacing and twirling around your
ankles and calves so your

frozen, afraid to trip
until feeding the beast becomes
irritating,
almost dangerous.

But today it's a white
crowned bird—a Polly want

Lost Birds

a cracker bird
and I remember my mother
trying to teach the parakeet to

Say "Pretty Edna" in the kitchen, face to the
wire birdcage.

which it never did. How she hated it's
cage and

on Saturdays we would let bird out
to fly around the house, then
try and find the shit

before my dad came home
sometimes
throwing already ironed

blouses back
into the washer to hide
the mess.

She grew tired of cleaning the cage, of
the bird's refusal to
do the one

thing she asked. One Saturday
in June
she left the cage door open
on the picnic table behind

the clothesline
hung with sheets.
For three days the blueness of his feathers
illuminated the pine
next door
And then, no more.

Was it her own tiny self
She saw in that bird?

Later when she was
demented wandering her acreage
I pulled into the driveway. She

met me, eyes full of concern.
We hid behind rhododendrons
cupping the dead sparrow

she removed from her
pocket.

We buried it together
then.
Her white hair flying in the wind

Modern Times

Alden Wallace

Modern Times in the city. Everyone is looking for love, even those who've already found it. Autumn leaves drift down from the boughs and their absence reveals a crescent moon huge and low on the cement horizon. A medium-sized dog leaps blindly, failing to catch a frisbee. A woman watches this from afar, baby clamped to her breast. In a coffee shop Yusef orders something new as he stares out at the people on the sidewalk, philosophizing on the difference between destination and direction, a reason unknowable and no reason at all. There's been a cloudy image on his mind for some time now. All throughout the pensive winter he has made progress in his craft by his own definition of the word. Now, as the fences of time have finally begun to lean, with pen to chin he smiles. Tonight, he says to the others, tonight we do what gods do.

The Best Days of My Life

Mishele Maron

Years before she sank on the Cornish coast, taking three of her crew members down with her, and long before Mark, my first captain in a decade aboard ships, was arrested for reckless endangerment of his crew, I spent three months aboard the world's oldest tall ship the *Maria Asumpta*, crisscrossing the English Channel.

I'd joined the ship surreptitiously after meeting one of the sailors in a port in Northern France, where I'd retreated after finishing my undergraduate studies in Paris. The sailor invited me down to see the ship, and after a rowdy tea hour with the crew, followed by a louder evening in a pub down the street, Captain Mark invited me to join them for a week. I stayed three months, and for a long while afterward, called those the best days of my life.

She was an all-wooden, classic Spanish brigantine. In order to set her sails, we climbed the rope ladders draping off her mast and sidled out along the yardarms, our legs dangling beneath us.

The first week aboard, while peeling potatoes, I dropped the paring knife and the blade landed in my right foot, sticking out gruesomely. What I remember now is the absence of pain. I'm tempted to say that there was pain, but that I didn't feel any. You have to be self-conscious to feel pain. And already, four days aboard, my self-awareness faced outwards, toward the sailors around me. All those voices with their curled accents—the engineer's Scottish brogue, the

Irish second mate's lilting cadence, clashing in their arguments about varnishing techniques, recipes, sea conditions, knots, and the punchline to jokes. They competed for my attention by singing sea shanties loudly.

It wasn't just the guys who were loud. The ship creaked. Ocean sloshed beneath us until it crested over the decks and across our boots. In the mornings, moored at port, the guys crowded into the table in the main saloon and I was surrounded again by the smells of aftershave, wood smoke, varnish, dust, mold, and salt—the fragrances mingling together to the point my eyes watered, and then someone cracked a joke or told a riddle or roasted someone and people laughed until they were breathless.

There is a scene in *The Odyssey* where Ulysses and his men eat the lotus flowers and become inebriated, losing all sense of mission and personal agency. I felt like that. As though I was floating in song, jokes, and laughter. At night, we gathered in a nearby dark-paneled pub, the only light in the establishment shining through half-emptied gin bottles—everyone toasting one another as they grew louder, happier, and drunker. To "eternal life," they said, raising their half-drained pint glasses.

Mark was an imposing figure, in possession of a Nordic face with high, chiseled cheekbones, flashing eyes. An aura of tossing seas and discipline about him. He'd been a captain in the British Royal Navy, and though I wasn't privy to the specifics of his career, a military officiousness ebbed off him. He stood slightly back inside himself and studied people and grunted to himself. Sometimes, when you tried to fix his attention, he'd turn away as though preoccupied. There were about nine guys and two women aboard when I joined—but people hopped off and on in a steady cadence that Mark facilitated in some mysterious manner.

There were always those who saw it as a privilege to be aboard and serve with Mark, especially the nautical students who saw him as the protectorate of nautical traditions.

Listening to him lead tourists around, speaking to a ship's chandlery, a paternal sort of pride underscoring his words when he said, "Well, of course, we see rough seas, she's seaworthy..." it seemed impossible that this was the same man who arose at 2a.m. to scream obscenities on the decks, but of course it was. In fact, that was the key to him, I now see, as a captain, he was also a master of ceremonies, manipulating tourists of their dollars, and crew of their work hours— our collective and respective resources funneled into a vision where nostalgia mingled with history, where the ship was akin to a gorgeous, if sorrowful woman it was our privilege to support.

Occasionally local journalists arrived to interview him, and Mark would strut around the decks, his posture stiff as a linguine noodle, his mouth snappish as he listed maritime facts, his British accent aristocratic sounding as an Oxford professor when he said, "She's the oldest working sailing ship in existence." But there was also the Mark who laughed gaily during mealtime when the guys told jokes, and the Mark who shamed anyone for wasting time, as our time belonged exclusively to the ship. "What in the bloody hell do you think I'm paying for?" he'd yell, at the guys smoking cigarettes. But since he barely paid anyone much, the guys just snickered.

Mark's contradictory nature would be a source of comic material. "Good old Mark," the sailors said, smirking knowingly, but being young, female, and American, I was somewhat removed from knowing why they snickered. Or what they knew of him. Or, any larger point.

There were stories about Mark back then. Rumor had it that before the *Maria Asumpta*, he'd captained a ship called the *Marques*, which sank in the mid-eighties during the *Cutty Sark* race to Halifax. At the time, the rumors were vague, but reading more about it recently, I learned that 19 of the 28 people aboard perished. An official inquiry found that the *Marques* had been unseaworthy because of a lack of stability.

Whatever I might have heard of this at the time, it had to compete with the immediacy of the ship, and the voices of the men drowning out my thoughts. Even tidbits of information that I might have heard about shipwrecks would be stuffs I failed to apply my own circumstances. Under the spell of the ship and the ocean, everything and everyone around were perceived through a glittery surrealness.

At twenty, and farther from home than I'd ever been, I likened international travel to Jackson Pollock's process of hurling paint at his cavasses. I'd left my rural Washington state home (a place most people didn't ever leave) for adventure, feeling a desperation to escape the pastures and catapult myself into the mysterious world around me. Once aboard the ship, I realized, that destinations mattered less than the journeying. Living aboard the *Maria* mirrored back to me things I could never have guessed about myself. How much I would love motoring towards an unknown coastline. How much I loved emerging from my cloistered, moldy-smelling bunk and hearing British voices arguing with one another in the main saloon. How much I would love not only the voices but the salt-tongued irreverence of the men telling absurd jokes. Growing up in a house plagued by a stepfather's mental illness, I'd habituated to filtering my every word and gesture to avoid triggering my stepfather's mood, and once exposed to the shipboard constant fun-making where I just wanted to bath in sloppy, salty British irreverence. All of this making it near impossible to process rumors I'd heard about prior shipwrecks and Mark's responsibility.

I didn't pay enough attention to the ship's mechanics to be a good deckhand. Deckhand duties required deft manipulation of her ropes and sails which I never understood.

The mate drew me a map of the rigging, with x's to specify where to stand if Mark said, "Portside tack," and even told me which ropes to grab, but still, I'd seize the wrong ropes. Or someone would hand me another rope connected to a part of the ship I hadn't yet learned about. As the newest member of the crew and one of three women, all of the men told me what to do, their instructions competing or conflicting. Mark would look at me and say something like, "Why is she just standing there?"

Captain Mark and the mate, Rex, ruled over the decks with a kind of Jekyll and Hyde routine. While Mark bellowed orders and sometimes insults such as "What in God's green earth are you holding that rope for?" at the top of his lungs. Rex, on the other hand, was always soft-spoken. Tall and broad-chested, and strong looking, he seemed to me like a nautical version of Superman's Clark Kent. The guys seemed to appreciate the rapport between the two men, as Mark bellowed orders and then people looked towards Rex, who'd nod to affirm or issue hand signal telling us to wait as he amended the plan.

What ultimately doomed my performance on the decks was a lack of respect for the ship. I was too young and immature to appreciate the ship as a living artifact. I wasn't a nautical student looking to clock sea miles for my certificate, and I wasn't an explorer biding my time as I plotted my winter trek to Antarctica. I was a fun-seeking renegade undergraduate student.

Which was just as well, as people cycled through habitually for one, or three, or six months stints. Mark didn't pay enough of a salary to keep anyone longer.

When the sailors on the *Maria* had first added me to their ranks, I talked passionately about the French language, how I'd planned to stay in France for an entire year, after which I'd return home, graduate, and apply to graduate schools where I could study the Ulysses story in greater depth. But they could see that I was jobless, disorganized, and my French embarrassingly halting and mispronounced.

When I joined the *Maria*, I assumed I'd return to France after a week, but within two days enjoying the shipboard sailing party my French ambitions dissolved into what they always had been, fantasies meant to fill a void which the ship quickly filled.

When I began to understand that everyone aboard had a specific skill set such as carpentry, navigation, ropes, or engineering, I knew needed to stop appearing like a buffoonish cartoon character on the decks. So, I reported to the galley.

The ship's cook, Phillipa, was a sunny young woman with buttery yellow hair and an infectious kindness that expanded around her like a cloud. Phillipa knew her way around the British classics she'd been raised on, but she wasn't an intuitive cook. Frankly, she didn't care for it. When I began making small improvements to the food, adding salt to the boiling potatoes, she nodded with appreciation used it as an excuse to sneak to the decks where she coiled ropes or climbed the mast to help the engineer with rope maintenance. With Phillipa taking longer and longer breaks, I found myself peeling potatoes on my own. One day, I beat eggs with cream and a can of golden syrup, a rich, British butterscotch flavored syrup to make a custardy bread pudding.

One lunchtime, I made three quiches, two with bacon and one with broccoli each with a flaky homemade crust. Captain Mark, who rarely addressed me directly, made eye contact at lunch, "Good work deserves notice," and raised his glass at me, and everyone said, "Here, here," which felt like a blessing.

Phillipa, setting her eyes on spending more time above decks, pitched to Mark that he should make me a regular crew member, and suddenly I was summoned to his cabin, descending the hole in the ship's stern via a steep ladder. It was the only time I'd ever be alone with Mark, his small, hooded eyes combing over me as though I was an interesting insect landing atop his antique sextant.

"You are a reliable cook," he said, his tone so condescending I didn't know how to respond and didn't. "I'd be happy to make you a more permanent member of the crew, except I couldn't possibly offer you any compensation..." He managed to pronounce the word *compensation* in a way that imbued the word with a hint of disgust, as though the money itself was an aberration.

Everyone aboard collected a small stipend. While I sorely needed funds, I just said, "Course, sir..." And though a week later, Mark began scheduling events which required food for 25, and 50 people, and hours of demanding work, I never complained. Instead, I saw the escalating demands as an invitation to expand my skill set. To make myself into a real cook. Besides the fact, cooking aboard a ship was fun. I'd do this until I got sick of it, I thought. Gallivanting between coastlines and recipes.

For most of the next ten years, I cooked aboard large yachts, crisscrossing the world. I fed millionaires and deckhands, and prepared fish so recently pulled from the Pacific their flesh was still warm. No more shepherd's pie for the *Maria*'s crew—now I was doing caviar service and ice sculptures. But in surprising ways, it never seemed that different to me. Potatoes or caviar, it all required the same skill set, a respect for ingredients, and appetites.

Rafts, yachts, ships, name the watery craft—now I can list the dangers. Three years from the *Maria*, I'd be aboard a 118-foot sailing yacht with a sailor whose sea experience compelled him to school his crew on safety protocols. Daily, for weeks, he forced me to roleplay rescue operations. Slow to absorb the details of man-overboard drills, he'd grow hawkish. "You don't understand. It will be me overboard. You'll be saving *me*. Now again!" He'd force me to throw out the life ring again until my arms ached. I learned how to pilot the yacht, release ropes from the hydraulic winches, and how to deploy the dozen types of emergency floatation devices.

Only then did I begin to appreciate how incredibly hazardous my stint aboard the *Maria* had been with all of the snappable ropes. The climbing into the rigging sans a harness.

No one warned me how, if a rope hit your neck at the right angle, your vertebrae would break like a pretzel. We didn't have lights in the rigging, judged by Mark as too modern. So, freighters couldn't see us in the world's busiest shipping channel. Worse yet: a wooden hull doesn't show up on a radar. When we crossed the Channel, one of the watch duties was to stand on the foredeck and hold a large flashlight aimed at the bow. Even I with no nautical knowledge understood that if any boat could see our light, we'd be too close to avert a collision. I asked the ship's engineer about this, who said, with his withering Scottish sarcasm, "Your point being?"

And my mouth snapped shut. I didn't mention anything safety-related again. The only thing worse than being the only American aboard was to be the American fraidy cat. And I flitted back to something funny one of the guys were doing. Or something I'd be cooking later. Or drinking in the beauty of the mist drifting across the green hills on the Cornish coastline, I'd think to myself, "But I'm so lucky."

I would get the news about *Maria*'s sinking three days after the accident. A sailor from the *Maria* I'd remained close with called me on a satellite phone. At the time, I was on the 118-foot sailing yacht with that safety-obsessed captain. The friend detailed everything he knew about the crash, which wasn't much.

Apparently, Mark had steered the ship closer than recommended to shore to get a photo opportunity. Mark's girlfriend was a professional photographer. I wondered if she was on the cliffside telling him to steer the ship closer?

I would read more about the incident later. How on the afternoon of May 30th, 1995, the *Maria Asumpta* was preparing to enter Padstow harbor when Mark decided to take her between the Mouls and Pentire Point (a route he'd been advised against), and apparently the engines stopped working.

Two crew were sent to attend to the engine while the rest of the fourteen crew raised more sail. Although lookouts had been posted at the bow, they failed to spot submerged rocks, and about five minutes after the engines stopped, *Maria* struck the coastline. The heavy swell carried her forward and then delivered her onto the coastline, where the 137-year old hull broke apart. This is the part I envision. The wooden hull cracking like an egg, its contents oozing into the spuming water. Eleven members of the crew including Mark himself scrambling onto the rocks, but three being swept away by waves and pronounced dead by drowning. This made Mark Litchfield responsible for the demise of two tall ships and the deaths of 21 people at sea. But on this second accident, there would be an investigation.

You can read about this online. A headline in the *Independent*, August 1997, reads, *Ship's Captain Jailed Over Crew Death on the Rocks.*

"Former Royal Navy lieutenant Mark Litchfield, 56, was found guilty on a majority decision at Exeter Crown Court after a five-week trial which followed the loss of the square-rigger on the north Cornwall coast."

Again, all of this information came to me years after the fact. When my friend called with the news, all we knew was the *Maria* was gone along with three crew members, none of whom were personally known to us but we couldn't help but feel as though we did know them. As though in some small way, those lives lost reflected something about us.

Accidents happen, we say. But when I said this at twenty, what I was really saying was that accidents happened to other people. To leave home is an act based upon hope that luck is on your side. But I wouldn't be able to identify that luck until I heard about *Maria* wrecking. During my time aboard the *Maria*, I learned a way of living that dictated the course of my life, for me then, my time aboard is labeled as some of the best days. For others though, it was their final days. When I think of the *Maria*, I think of this and for a few interminable seconds, life is precious again, until that too fades.

When One Thing Stands

Madronna Holden

When one thing stands, another stands beside it.

—Igbo proverb

I
When one thing stands,
another stands beside it.

When elders lift up their hearts
children walk upright
into their years.

For every ugliness a hidden beauty.

For every face pressed against the door
a way in.

For every mote of dust,
there is a wind that blows it.

For every land, its own sky.

II

Inanna, Queen of Morning,
hears the call of Ereshkigal,
Queen of Night, from her house
of hems and roots.

Spinning thread,
whorl of the universe
what thing is she not
with her sister by her side?

She is the rock designing water,
the softened stone that falls
through time, rescued
by earth and moss.

Against the desert
she is the rain of blood,
against the flood she is
drinking, believing.

She is the bull begun
in the horn of Africa,
the owl and the seed,
the eyes of the stars that
oversee the night.

When one thing stands,
another stands beside it.

When you rise,
I rise with you.

Trees everywhere
grow closer to heaven.

Symphony at Powell Butte

Suzy Harris

I hear wind dance in tall grasses
and earth's slow rotation.
I hear clouds gliding above
and unnamed birds chittering in trees.
I hear rocks murmuring to each other,
reminiscing about the old days
when they were once part of something bigger.
I hear our dog asking for water
as we climb the last hill before the forested path
opens to wide-open grassland,
then earth again in its lurch forward.

Contributors

A native of New York State and now long-time New Orleanian, **Christina Albers** has taught college, high school, and even pre-school while occasionally writing, with one book published (on Henry James's short stories) along with a small handful of articles, essays, and letters to the editor and one previous poem in *St. Ann's Review*. Currently she works in the writing center at Delgado Community College in New Orleans.

Jeffrey Alfier's most recent book, *The Shadow Field*, was published by Louisiana Literature Journal & Press (2020). His lit journal credits include *The Carolina Quarterly, Copper Nickel, Hotel Amerika, James Dickey Review, New York Quarterly, Southern Poetry Review*, and *Vassar Review*.

Nathan Bas is a CCC and PSU graduate with publications in *Polaris* and the *Clackamas Literary Review*. He still resides in Oregon City, Oregon, working as a pet-sitter and plays with poems.

Patrick Browne is an emerging author, currently working on his first novel. His literary passions tend toward magical realism and speculative fiction, and he is particularly interested in imaginative exploration of the natural world. He is also a higher education administrator at him alma mater, New York University, where he works on global strategic partnerships. Raised in New Jersey, he currently lives in Staten Island, New York, with his husband, musician Garuda Grey.

Aleksandra Byrska edited the cultural magazine *Fragile* and is the author of the play *Śnieg [Snow]* published in the anthology *Nasz głos [Our Voice]* by the Helena Modrzejewska National Stary Theater in Kraków. Recent poems of hers have appeared in *Tlen Literacki*, *Biuro Literackie*, *Mały Format*, *Wakat*, and, in English translation, *La Piccioletta Barca*, *Periodicities*, and *Salt Hill*. She is a librarian, Polish language teacher, and speech therapist.

At 82, it is the peace in **Andrea Campbell's** heart to translate the activities of the world into some kind of beauty. Her teacher, Thich Nhat Hanh, tells Andrea that her true home is in the here and now and that is where she will rest. She currently lives in SE Portland, Oregon.

William Cass has had over 250 short stories accepted for publication in a variety of literary magazines such as *december*, *Briar Cliff Review*, and *Zone 3*. He was a finalist in short fiction and novella competitions at *Glimmer Train* and Black Hill Press, and won writing contests at Terrain.org and *The Examined Life Journal*. He has received one Best Small Fictions nomination, three Pushcart nominations, and his short story collection, *Something Like Hope & Other Stories*, was recently released by Wising Up Press. He lives in San Diego, California.

Emma Charlton spends most of her time crocheting for her small business, Alaska Crochet. Last spring, she graduated with her English degree from The University of Alaska Fairbanks, where she worked as Editor in Chief on their literary journal. Her nonfiction and poetry have been published in *Ice Box*, *The Albion Review*, *Prairie Margins*, and *North Dakota Quarterly*.

Marisa P. Clark is a queer writer whose prose and poetry appear or are forthcoming in *Shenandoah, Cream City Review, Nimrod, Epiphany, Foglifter, Rust + Moth, Texas Review, Folio,* and elsewhere. *The Best American Essays 2011* recognized her creative nonfiction among its Notable Essays. A fiction reader for *New England Review,* she hails from the South and lives in the Southwest with three parrots, two dogs, and whatever wildlife and strays stop to visit.

Grace Cram is a freelance writer and poet. Born and raised in Minnesota, she holds much love for the Midwest but loves her new residence in South Florida just a little more. She has two poems published in both the *Living Waters Review* and *The Sailfish Review,* a poem forthcoming in *Saw Palm: Florida Literature & Art,* and four poems forthcoming in *Euphemism.* She is generally inspired by walks along the intercoastal and drives up the coast. Propelled by a love of words—and iced coffee—she spends her days reading and writing in between trips to the beach and shifts at her local smoothie shop.

Allison A. deFreese's translations of Karla Marrufo's work have previously appeared in *Apofenie, Los Angeles Review, New England Review, SAND Journal Berlin,* and *Your Impossible Voice.* Her translation of the book in which this excerpt appears is forthcoming from Dalkey Archive Press in 2023. She teaches at Clackamas Community College in Oregon City, Oregon.

Justin Duyao is a critic, writer and editor pursing an MA in Critical Studies from the Pacific Northwest College of Art. He holds degrees in English Literature, French, and Religious Thought from Harding University and has published in *Oregon ArtsWatch, Variable*

West, *Weathered*, and *Dismantle Magazine*. He lives in Portland, Oregon.

Sarah Kain Gutowski is the author of *Fabulous Beast: Poems* (Texas Review Press), winner of the 14th annual National Indies Excellence Award for Poetry. Her poems have appeared in various print and on-line journals, including the *Gettysburg Review*, *Threepenny Review*, *Painted Bride Quarterly*, and *The Southern Review*. Her criticism has been published most recently in *Colorado Review* (online), *The New York Journal of Books*, and *Calyx: A Journal of Art and Literature by Women*.

Suzy Harris is a retired attorney who has rediscovered her love of poetry. Her work has recently been published in *Cirque*, *Switchgrass Review*, *Timberline Review*, and *Williwaw Journal*. She lives in Portland, Oregon.

Phil Harvey has been published in numerous magazines, including *Antietam Review*, *The Erotic Review*, *The MacGuffin*, and over twenty others. His writing has received several honors, including a Pushcart nomination. Harvey is the founder and chairman of DKT International, a nonprofit family planning and AIDS prevention organization, and president of the company Adam & Eve.

Madronna Holden is using the time afforded her by recent retirement from teaching to focus on her award-winning poetry. Besides the appearance of her work in two previous issues of *Clackamas Literary Review*, over fifty of her poems have appeared in *The Christian Science Monitor*, *The Cold Mountain Review*, *The Bitter Oleander*, *Puerto del*

Sol, *Leaping Clear*, and many others. One of her poems was recently featured as poem of the day on Verse Daily, and a documentary on the production of her full length poetry drama, *The Descent of Inanna*, was aired on Oregon Public Broadcasting. Her chapbook, *Goddess of Glass Mountains*, was published from Finishing Line Press (2021).

Anne Holub's poetry has been featured on Chicago Public Radio and in *The Doubleback Review*, *The Mississippi Review*, *The Asheville Poetry Review*, *Phoebe*, and *The Beacon Street Review*, among other publications, and in the anthology *Bright Bones: Contemporary Montana Writing*, (Open Country Press, 2018). Her first chapbook, *27 Threats to Everyday Life*, is forthcoming from Finishing Line Press. She received a MFA from the University of Montana and a MA from Hollins University. Originally from Charlottesville, Virginia, she now lives and writes in Montana with her husband Dan, their two dogs Merle and Rosie, and a sourdough starter named Rhonda.

Bronwyn Hughes is a certified public accountant currently working on her MFA in creative writing from Randolph College. She enjoys beekeeping, filmmaking, and boating on the many creeks and rivers feeding the Chesapeake Bay. Bronwyn lives in Tidewater, Virginia, with her partner and a Maine coon cat. Her work has appeared in *Atherton Review* and *Evening Street Review*.

Poet and songwriter **Paul Ilechko** lives with his partner in Lambertville, New Jersey. He is the author of several chapbooks. His work has appeared in a variety of journals, including *The Night Heron Barks*, *Feral Journal*, *Iron Horse Literary Review*, *Gargoyle Magazine*, and *Book of Matches*. His first album, *Meeting Points*, was released in 2021.

Harvey James is a freelance writer based in South East London, UK. His features have appeared in *VICE*, *Wired*, *British GQ*, *HIGHS-NOBIETY* covering fashion, technology, and culture. Meanwhile, his short stories have been featured in *Adelaide Magazine* and *The Daily Drunk Magazine* covering tackle tech, culture, and life with a pinch of humour.

Morgan Jeitler is a senior at the University of Texas at Austin studying English and Plan II Honors. She has previously been published in *Hothouse Literary Journal* and won an honorable mention in the writing flag award at her university.

Jeffrey N. Johnson's story collection, *Other Fine Gifts*, won an Ippy Award silver medal for Best Regional Fiction: Mid-Atlantic, and his novel, *The Hunger Artist*, was a finalist for the Library of Virginia's People's Choice Award. *The Sewanee Review* awarded him the Andrew Lytle Fiction Prize for best short story of 2011. His fiction and poetry have appeared in *Birmingham Poetry Review*, *The Carolina Quarterly*, *Clackamas Literary Review*, *Evansville Review*, *Gargoyle*, *Lake Effect*, *Real: Regarding Arts and Letters*, *Red Rock Review*, *Roanoke Review*, *South Carolina Review*, *Santa Clara Review*, and *War, Literature and the Arts*. His play, *Affair at the Hotel Opal*, had a full production at the Potomac Players 4th Annual One-Act Festival in Hagerstown, Maryland. He is a fellow of the Virginia Center for the Creative Arts and a recipient of a Creative Fellow grant from the Mid-Atlantic Arts Foundation.

Joe Johnson writes fiction and poetry. His work has appeared in *Flash*, *Heron Tree*, *Rust + Moth*, *Aethlon*, and *The Santa Clara Review*, among others. He has won the Editor's Choice Award for *Carve Magazine*, was a finalist for *Fiction Southeast's* Ernest Hemingway Flash Fiction Prize and for the Ruby Irene Poetry Chapbook Contest, and was a semi-finalist for the St. Lawrence Book Award. He is a graduate of the Rainier Writing Workshop at Pacific Lutheran University.

Katie Lynn Johnston is a creative writing graduate of Columbia College Chicago. They have been an editor for the *Columbia Poetry Review*, *Mulberry Literary*, and a production editor for *Hair Trigger Magazine*. Their work has appeared in *Allium*, *Hoxie Gorge Review*, *Lavender Review*, among others, and their essay, "The Barriers Faced by Female Writers," was published on the *Fountainhead Press* website and won the Excellence Award at the Student Writers' Showcase.

Mercedes Lawry is the author of three chapbooks, the latest, *In the Early Garden with Reason*, was selected by Molly Peacock for the 2018 WaterSedge Chapbook Contest. Her poetry has appeared in such journals as *Poetry*, *Nimrod*, and *Prairie Schooner* and has been nominated seven times for a Pushcart Prize.

Sue Fagalde Lick, who lives in Newport, Oregon, has published two chapbooks, *Gravel Road Ahead* and *The Widow at the Piano: Poems by a Distracted Catholic*. Her poems have appeared in *Rattle*, *The MacGuffin*, *Willawaw*, *Cloudbank*, *New Letters*, *The American Journal of Poetry*, and other publications. She returned to poetry after many years working as a journalist in the Bay Area, earning her MFA in creative writing at Antioch University Los Angeles at age 51. When not writing, she leads an alternate life as a music minister.

Mishele Maron is a writer living in Seattle, Washington. She is a graduate of Cooking School of the Rockies culinary program, and obtained her MFA from Rainier Writer's Workshop. Her work has recently appeared in the online zine *Detour Ahead*, and the *Awakenings Review*. She is currently finishing a memoir entitled, *If You Can Cook, You Can Stay*, about her decade long career in the food industry.

Karla Marrufo (Mérida, México) holds a Doctorate in Hispanic-American Literature from la Universidad Veracruzana. Her work in Spanish has been recognized through several prestigious literary awards, among them: Mexico's National Dolores Castro Prize for Women, the National Wilberto Cantón Award in Playwriting, the XVI José Díaz Bolio Poetry Prize, a postdoctoral fellowship from the UNAM, and a fellowship from the Program for the Expansion and Development of Creativity and the Arts in the Yucatán. She is the author of seven books, including plays, works of poetry, fiction, nonfiction, and literary criticism.

Steven Mayer is an old man and young writer who lives on Oregon's North Coast. He wanders beaches in warm months, watches winter storms during cold months, and hangs out in coffee shops with friends. His passion is storytelling, memoir, and prose. He authored *Finding Heart* (2012) and *Finding More Heart* (2018). His poetry and prose appear in various journals.

Cassidy McCants received her B.A. in creative writing from University of Arkansas and her M.F.A. in fiction writing at Vermont College of Fine Arts. She edits for *Nimrod Journal* and *Through the Fire* and is creator/editor of *Apple in the Dark*. Her prose has appeared in or is forthcoming from *The Lascaux Review, Liars' League NYC, Gravel, The Idle Class, filling Station, Witch Craft Magazine, Grist,* and other publications. She won the 2020 Innovative Short Fiction Contest from *The Conium Review,* and her stories have received honorable mentions from *Glimmer Train Press.* She is a 2020 Artist INC fellow.

Kayla Meyers is a 33 year old artist and writer living in West Linn, Oregon, with her family and animals. She first began painting in August of 2019.

A retired high school English teacher, **Cecil Morris** divides his time between Oregon and California. He has poems appearing in *2River View, Cobalt Review, Ekphrastic Review, Evening Street Review, Hole in the Head Review, Midwest Quarterly,* and *Talking River Review.* He enjoys ice cream too much and cruciferous vegetables too little for his own good.

Greg Nicholl's poetry has most recently appeared or is forthcoming in *Harpur Palate, Hawai'i Pacific Review, North American Review, Sugar House Review, West Branch,* and elsewhere. He is a four-time Pushcart Prize nominee and a freelance editor currently living in Boston.

Shilo Niziolek's nonfiction manuscript, *Fever,* was first runner-up in Red Hen Press's Quill Prose Prize and a finalist in *Zone 3 Press's* 2021 CNF Award. Her writing has appeared in *[PANK], Juked, Entropy, HerStry, Oregon Humanities,* among others, and is forthcoming in Pork Belly Press's zine: *Love Me, Love My Belly.* Shilo holds an MFA from New England College and is a writing instructor at Clackamas Community

College in Oregon City, Oregon. She is currently seeking homes for her nonfiction manuscript, *Fever*, and her poetry collection, *Atrophy*.

Robert K. Omura calls Calgary, Alberta, Canada, home where he lives with his common law wife and three too many cats. He has resigned himself to finding cat fur in everything he eats. His fiction and poetry appears or is forthcoming in journals in the U.S., Canada, and abroad including the *New York Quarterly*, *34thParallel*, *barnstorm*, *Copperfield Review*, *Brink*, and *Blue Skies Poetry*. He has been nominated for the Pushcarts.

Konstantinos Patrinos is an aspiring writer based in Berlin, Germany. His work has appeared or is forthcoming in *Rust + Moth*, *Pinyon*, *California Quarterly*, *Toyon*, *Paris Lit Up*, *Door Is A Jar*, *Open Minds Quarterly*, and others. When he's not writing poetry, he enjoys getting punched in the face during kickboxing classes. He's a high school teacher for political science and philosophy.

Vivienne Popperl lives in Portland, Oregon. Her poems have appeared in *Clackamas Literary Review*, *Timberline Review*, *Cirque*, *Rain Magazine*, *About Place Journal*, and other publications. She was poetry co-editor for the Fall 2017 edition of *VoiceCatcher*. She received both second place and anhonorable mention in the 2021 Kay Snow awards poetry category by WillametteWriters. Her first book, *A Nest in the Heart*, is forthcoming by The Poetry Box.

Originally from the suburbs of New Jersey, **Ken Post** worked for the Forest Service in Alaska for 40 years, including many seasons on a million-acre island with more brown bears than there are people. He writes short stories during the long, dark winters. Ken's fiction has previously appeared in *Cirque*, *Red Fez*, *Underwood Press*, *Poor Yorick*, and is forthcoming in *Kansas City Voices* and *Woven Tale Press*. His story, "Enola Gay," published in *Red Fez*, was nominated for a Pushcart Prize in 2020.

Jeanne Rana has been published in *Apricity Magazine*, *Fresh Rain*, *Blood Tree Literature*, *Marin Poetry Center Anthology*, *Feather River Bulletin*, *Earth's Daughters*, *Edison Literary Review*, *Flights*, *Paterson Literary Review*, and *Ponder Review*. She received a Poets & Writers grant for her performance and workshop in 2019 for the Plumas Arts Council in Quincy, California. She worked as a high school English and American history teacher for twenty-five years before becoming an acquisitions editor for Hunter House Publishers. Jeanne sings Sufi devotionals and runs a Sufi center with her husband.

Laura Remington lives and writes in Northern California, but at heart she's a Yooper, born and raised in the Upper Peninsula of Michigan. *Jabberwock Review* turned her into a published writer, and her fiction has since appeared in several publications, including *Barstow & Grand*, *Third Wednesday*, and *Dash*.

Kan Ren Jie is a Singaporean writer, currently based in Shanghai. His poems have been previously featured or are forthcoming in the *Bellevue Literary Review*, *Yalobusha Review*, *Contrary Magazine*, and *Spittoon Monthly*.

Kristel Rietesel-Low received her MFA in Poetry from the University of Illinois at Urbana-Champaign. Her work has appeared or is forthcoming in *The Briar Cliff Review*, *The National Poetry Review*, *South Dakota Review*, *Cimarron Review*, *Shenandoah*, and elsewhere. She lives in the San Francisco Bay Area.

Maureen Sherbondy's work has appeared in *The Stone Canoe*, *Wigleaf*, *Upstreet*, *Calyx*, and other journals. *Lucky Brilliant*, her young adult novel, was published in 2020. *Lines in Opposition* will be published in April by Unsolicited Press. Maureen lives in Durham, North Carolina.

Connie Soper is a hard-core Oregonian who writes poems in her head while she's hiking or beachcombing. She has recently come back to poetry after a long hiatus and is trying to make up for lost time. She divides her time between Portland and Manzanita, Oregon, and is continually inspired by the time she spends at the Oregon Coast. Connie Soper's poems have recently appeared in *North Coast Squid*, *Catamaran*, *The Ekphrastic Review*, *Windfall*, and *Rain Magazine*. Publication of her first full-length book of poetry is forthcoming in 2022 from Airlie Press.

Richard Stimac published poetry in *Burningword*, *Faultline*, *Havik* (2021 Best in Show for Poetry), *Michigan Quarterly Review*, *Penumbra*, *Salmon Creek Journal*, *Wraparound South*, and others, and an article on Willa Cather in *The Midwest Quarterly*.

Saramanda Swigart has a BA in postcolonial literature and an MFA in writing and literary translation from Columbia University. Her short work, essays, and poetry have appeared in *Oxford Magazine*, *Superstition Review*, *The Alembic*, *Fogged Clarity*, *Ghost Town*, *The*

Saranac Review, and *Euphony* to name a few. She has been teaching literature, creative writing, and argumentative writing and critical thinking at City College of San Francisco since 2014.

Mark Tardi is a writer, translator, and lecturer on faculty at the University of Łódź. He is a recipient of a 2022 NEA Fellowship in Translation and the author of three books, most recently, *The Circus of Trust* (Dalkey Archive, 2017). Recent work and translations have appeared in *Lunch Ticket, The Scores, Denver Quarterly, The Millions, Circumference, La Piccioletta Barca, Jet Fuel Review, Berlin Quarterly*, and in Italian translation, *Rossocorpolingua*. His translations of *The Squatters' Gift* by Robert Rybicki (Dalkey Archive) and *Faith in Strangers* by Katarzyna Szaulińska (Toad Press/Veliz Books) were published in 2021.

Miles Waggener is the author of four volumes of poetry: *Phoenix Suites, Sky Harbor, Desert Center*, and most recently *Superstition Freeway*, published by The Word Works of Washington, DC. He has been the recipient of The Washington Prize as well as individual grants from the Arizona Commission on the Arts and the Nebraska Arts Council. He heads the writing program at the University of Nebraska at Omaha, where he has been a faculty member since 2006.

Cheryl Waitkevich is a recently retired person, lives in Olympia, Washington, and right now is watching the wind come in from the south as its haggles with the curly willow in her front yard. She/they has been published in *Cirque, Spindrift* and *The Galway Review* and hopes to continue writing fiction and poetry for as long as stories show themselves.

Alden Wallace has been published in literary magazines around the world. He is the author of a chapbook of poetry entitled *Endless Nights*.

Michael Washburn is a Brooklyn-based writer and journalist and the author of four short story collections. His story "Confessions of a Spook" won Causeway Lit's 2018 fiction contest, and another of his stories, "In the Flyover State," was named a Distinguished Mystery Story of 2014 by *The Best American Mystery Stories*.

John Sibley Williams is the author of nine poetry collections, including *Scale Model of a Country at Dawn* (Cider Press Review Poetry Award), *The Drowning House* (Elixir Press Poetry Award), *As One Fire Consumes Another* (Orison Poetry Prize), *Skin Memory* (Backwaters Prize, University of Nebraska Press), and *Summon* (JuxtaProse Chapbook Prize). His book *Sky Burial: New & Selected Poems* is forthcoming in translated form by the Portuguese press do lado esquerdo. A twenty-seven-time Pushcart nominee, John is the winner of numerous awards, including the Wabash Prize for Poetry, Philip Booth Award, Phyllis Smart-Young Prize, and Laux/Millar Prize. He serves as editor of *The Inflectionist Review* and founder of the Caesura Poetry Workshop series. Previous publishing credits include *Best American Poetry*, *Yale Review*, *Verse Daily*, *North American Review*, *Prairie Schooner*, and *TriQuarterly*.

Elizabeth Wood is a writer, educator, and visual artist. She lives and works in Montreal, Canada.

The *Clackamas Literary Review* is typeset in Sabon LT Std, an old-style serif designed by Jan Tschichold, and in Optima, a humanistic sans-serif designed by Hermann Zapf, and printed on 50 lb. creme paper. Editing and design done by English Department students and faculty at Clackamas Community College, in Oregon City, Oregon.

Visit

CLR

CLACKAMAS LITERARY REVIEW

clackamasliteraryreview.org
clackamasliteraryreview.submittable.com
facebook.com/clackamasliteraryreview
@clackamaslitrev

Contact
clr@clackamas.edu

CLACKAMAS LITERARY REVIEW

the finest writing for the best readers

Clackamas Literary Review has been committed to publishing quality writing from around the world since 1997. Use the form below or visit us on Submittable to receive the latest and forthcoming issues.

Clackamas Literary Review

_____	1 year	$12
_____	2 years	$22
_____	3 years	$32

Name _____

Address _____

City / State / Zip _____

Email _____

Send this form and check or money order to:

Clackamas Literary Review
English Department
Clackamas Community College
19600 Molalla Avenue
Oregon City, Oregon 97045

www.ingramcontent.com/pod-product-compliance
Lightning Source LLC
Chambersburg PA
CBHW021953190626
46807CB00005BB/2248

9781732033344